The **...h** *ana* **...al.**

Parks chased after it before it dropped into the crowd of baseball fans. Sitting on the third base line, Brooke found herself face-to-face with him. Their eyes met again, but she didn't move—partly because she was paralyzed.

Parks stared back at her. "Your name?" he demanded.

He had that fierce, dangerous look on his face again. Brooke schooled her voice to calmness. "Brooke."

"All of it, damn it," Parks muttered, pressed for time and furious with himself.

"Gordon," Brooke told him smoothly. "Is the game over?"

Parks narrowed his eyes before he moved away. "It's just beginning."

Dear Reader:

There is an electricity between two people in love that makes everything they do magic, larger than life. This is what we bring you in SILHOUETTE INTIMATE MOMENTS.

SILHOUETTE INTIMATE MOMENTS are longer, more sensuous romance novels filled with adventure, suspense, glamor or melodrama. These books have an element no one else has tapped: excitement.

We are proud to present the very best romance has to offer from the very best romance writers. In the coming months look for some of your favorite authors such as Elizabeth Lowell, Nora Roberts, Erin St. Claire and Brooke Hastings.

SILHOUETTE INTIMATE MOMENTS are for the woman who wants more than she has ever had before. These books are for you.

Karen Solem
Editor-in-Chief
Silhouette Books

Rules Of The Game

Nora Roberts

Silhouette Intimate Moments
Published by Silhouette Books New York
America's Publisher of Contemporary Romance

SILHOUETTE BOOKS, a Division of Simon & Schuster, Inc.
1230 Avenue of the Americas, New York, N.Y. 10020

Copyright © 1984 by Nora Roberts
Cover artwork copyright © 1984 Lisa Falkenstern

Distributed by Pocket Books

ISBN: 0-671-50299-9

First Silhouette Books printing October, 1984

10 9 8 7 6 5 4 3 2 1

America's Publisher of Contemporary Romance

Printed in the U.S.A.

Books by Nora Roberts

Silhouette Romance

Silhouette Special Edition

Silhouette Intimate Moments

Pocket Books

For Dan,
who loves the game.

Rules
Of The Game

Chapter 1

"A JOCK. TERRIFIC." BROOKE TOOK A LONG SWALLOW of strong black coffee, tipped back in her glove-soft leather chair and scowled. "I love it."

"No need to be sarcastic," Claire returned mildly. "If de Marco wants to use an athlete for promotion, why should you object?" She gazed absently at the chunky gold ring on her right hand. "After all," Claire continued in her dry voice, "you'll be making quite a bit directing the commercials."

Brooke sent Claire a characteristic look. Direct, uncompromising gray eyes bored into the soft blue of the older woman's. One of Brooke's greatest talents, and her greatest weapons, was her ability to stare down anyone from a corporate president to a temperamental actor. She'd developed the knack early as a defense against her own insecurity and had since refined it to an art. It was an art, however, that didn't impress Claire Thorton. At

11

forty-nine, she was the head of a multimillion-dollar company that she'd started with brains and guts. For nearly a quarter of a century, she had run things her way, and she intended to keep right on doing so.

She'd known Brooke for ten years—since Brooke had been an eighteen-year-old upstart who had wheedled her way into a job with Thorton Productions. Then she'd watched Brooke work her way up from gofer to gaffer, from gaffer to assistant cameraman and from there to director. Claire had never regretted the impulse that had led her to give Brooke her first fifteen-second commercial.

Intuition had been the basis for Claire's success with Thorton Productions, and intuitively she had sensed sharp talent in Brooke Gordon. In addition, Claire knew her, understood her, as few others did. Perhaps it was because they shared two basic traits—ambition and independence.

After a moment, Brooke gave up with a sigh. "A jock," she muttered again as she gazed around her office.

It was one small room, the pale-amber walls lined with prints of stills from dozens of her commercials. There was a two-cushion sofa—reupholstered in chocolate-colored corduroy—not comfortable enough to encourage long visits. The chair with a tufted back had been picked up at a yard sale along with a coffee table that leaned slightly to the left.

Brooke sat behind an old, scarred desk that had a drawer that wouldn't quite close. On it were piles of papers, a gooseneck lamp and assorted disposable pens and broken pencils. The pens and pencils were jammed in a Sevres vase. Behind her at the window, a dieffenbachia was slowly dying in an exquisitely worked pottery bowl.

"Damn, Claire, why can't they get an actor?" Brooke tossed up her hands in her one theatrical gesture, then dropped her chin on them. "Do you know what it's like to try to coax ball players and rock stars to say a line without freezing or hamming it up?" With a disgusted mutter that gave no room for comment, she pushed the pile of papers into a semiordered heap. "One call to a casting agent and I could have a hundred qualified actors parading through here itching for the job."

Patiently, Claire brushed a speck of lint from the sleeve of her rose linen suit. "You know it increases sales if a production's hyped by a recognizable name or familiar face."

"Recognizable name?" Brooke tossed back. "Who's ever heard of Parks Jones? *Stupid* name," she muttered to herself.

"Every baseball fan in the country." The mild smile told Brooke it was useless to argue. Therefore, she prepared to argue further.

"We're selling clothes, not Louisville Sluggers."

"Eight Golden Gloves," Claire went on. "A lifetime batting average of three twenty-five. He's leading the league in RBIs this season. Jones has been at third base in the All-Star game for eight consecutive seasons."

Brooke narrowed her eyes. "How do you know so much? You don't follow baseball."

"I do my homework." A cool smile touched Claire's round, pampered face. She'd never had a face-lift but was religious about her visits to Elizabeth Arden. "That's why I'm a successful producer. Now you'd better do yours." She rose languidly. "Don't make any plans, I've got tickets for the game tonight. Kings against the Valiants.''

"Who?"

"Do your homework," Claire advised before she closed the office door behind her.

With an exasperated oath, Brooke swiveled her chair around so that she faced her view of Los Angeles—tall buildings, glittering glass and clogged traffic. She'd had other views of L.A. during the rise in her career, but they'd been closer to street level. Now, she looked out on the city from the twentieth floor. The distance meant success, but Brooke didn't dwell on it. To do that would have encouraged thinking of the past—something Brooke meticulously avoided.

Leaning back in the oversized chair, Brooke toyed with the end of her braid. Her hair was the warm soft red shot with gold that painters attempted to immortalize. It was long and thick and unruly. Brooke was feminine enough not to want it cut to a more manageable length and practical enough to subdue it into a fat braid during working hours. It hung down the back of a thin silk blouse past the waistband of overworked blue jeans.

Her eyes as she mulled over Claire's words were thoughtful. They had misty gray irises, long lids and were surrounded by lashes in the same fragile shade as her hair. She rarely thought to darken them. Her skin was the delicate ivory-rose her hair demanded but the frailty stopped there. Her nose was small and sharp, her mouth wide, her chin aggressive. It was an unsettling face—beautiful one moment, austere the next, but always demanding. She wore a hasty dab of rose lipstick, enameled dimestore earrings and a splash of two-hundred-dollar-an-ounce perfume.

She thought about the de Marco account—designer jeans, exclusive sportswear and soft Italian leather. Since they'd decided to move their advertising beyond the glossy pages of fashion magazines and into television, they had come to Thorton Productions, and so to her. It was a fat two-year contract with a budget that would give Brooke all the artistic room she could want. She told herself she deserved it. There were three Clios on the corner shelf to her right.

Not bad, she mused, for a twenty-eight-year-old woman who had walked into Thorton Productions with a high school diploma, a glib tongue and sweaty palms. And twelve dollars and fifty-three cents in her pocket, Brooke remembered; then she pushed the thought aside. If she wanted the de Marco account—and she did—she would simply have to make the ball player work. Grimly, she swung her chair back to face her desk. Picking up the phone, Brooke punched two buttons.

"Get me everything we have on Parks Jones," she ordered as she shuffled papers out of her way. "And ask Ms. Thorton what time I'm to pick her up tonight."

Less than six blocks away, Parks Jones stuck his hands in his pockets and scowled at his agent. "How did I ever let you talk me into this?"

Lee Dutton gave a smile that revealed slightly crooked teeth and a lot of charm. "You trust me."

"My first mistake." Parks studied Lee, a not quite homely, avuncular figure with a receding hairline, puckish face and unnerving black eyes. Yes, he trusted him, Parks thought, he even liked the shrewd little devil, but . . . "I'm not a damn model, Lee, I'm a third baseman."

"You're not modeling," Lee countered. As he folded his hands, the sun glinted on the band of his thin Swiss watch. "You're endorsing. Ball players have been doing it since the first razor blade."

Parks snorted then walked around the tidy, Oriental-designed office. "This isn't a shaving commercial, and I'm not endorsing a mitt. It's clothes, for God's sake. I'm going to feel like an idiot."

But you won't look like one, Lee thought as he drew out a fragrant, slim cigar. Lighting it, he studied Parks over the flame. The long, lanky body was perfect for de Marco's—as was the blond, unmistakably California look. Parks's tanned lean face, navy-blue eyes and tousled curling hair had already made him a favorite with the female fans, while his friendly, laid-back charm had won over the men. He was talented, easy to look at and personable. In short, Lee concluded, he was a natural. The fact that he was intelligent was at times as much a disadvantage as an advantage.

"Parks, you're hot." Lee said it with a sigh that they both knew was calculated. "You're also thirty-three. How much longer are you going to play ball?"

Parks answered with a glare. Lee knew of his vow to retire at thirty-five. "What does that have to do with it?"

"There are a lot of ball players, exceptional ball players, who slip into oblivion when they walk off the diamond for the last time. You have to think of the future."

"I *have* thought of the future," Parks reminded him. "Maui—fishing, sleeping in the sun, ogling women."

That would last about six weeks, Lee calculated, but he wisely kept silent.

"Lee." Parks flopped into a Chinese-red chair and

stretched out his legs. "I don't need the money. So why am I going to be working this winter instead of laying on the beach?"

"Because it's going to be good for you," Lee began. "It's good for the game. The campaign will enhance the image of baseball. And," he added with one of his puckish smiles, "because you signed a contract."

"I'm going to get in some extra batting practice," Parks muttered as he rose. When he reached the door, he turned back with a suspiciously friendly smile. "One thing. If I make a fool of myself, I'm going to break the legs on your Tang horse."

Brooke screeched through the electronically controlled gates then swerved up the rhododendron-lined drive that led to Claire's mansion. Privately, Brooke considered it a beautiful anachronism. It was huge, white, multileveled and pillared. Brooke liked to imagine two black-helmeted guards, rifles on shoulders, flanking the carved double doors. The estate had originally belonged to a silent movie idol who had supposedly decked out the rooms in pastel silks and satins. Fifteen years before, Claire had purchased it from a perfume baron and had proceeded to redecorate it with her own passion for Oriental art.

Brooke stomped on the brake of her Datsun, screaming to a halt in front of the white marble stairs. She drove at two speeds: stop and go. Stepping out of the car, she breathed in the exotic garden scents of vanilla and jasmine before striding up the stairs in the loose-limbed gait that came from a combination of long legs and preoccupation. In a crowd, her walk would cause men's heads to turn but Brooke neither noticed nor cared.

She knocked briskly on the door, then impatiently tried the handle. Finding it unlocked, she walked into the spacious mint-green hall and shouted.

"Claire! Are you ready? I'm starving." A neat little woman in a tailored gray uniform came through a doorway to the left. "Hello, Billings." Brooke smiled at her and tossed her braid over her shoulder. "Where's Claire? I haven't the energy to search through this labyrinth for her."

"She's dressing, Ms. Gordon." The housekeeper spoke in modulated British tones, responding to Brooke's smile with a nod. "She'll be down shortly. Would you care for a drink?"

"Just some Perrier, it's muggy out." Brooke followed the housekeeper into the drawing room then slumped down on a divan. "Did she tell you where we're going?"

"To a baseball game, miss?" Billings set ice in a glass and added sparkling water. "Some lime?"

"Just a squirt. Come on, Billings." Brooke's smoky contralto became conspiratorial. "What do you think?"

Billings meticulously squeezed lime into the bubbly water. She'd been housekeeper for Lord and Lady Westbrook in Devon before being prized away by Claire Thorton. On accepting the position, she had vowed never to become Americanized. Edna Billings had her standards. But she'd never quite been able to resist responding to Brooke. A naughty young girl, she'd thought a decade before, and the opinion remained unchanged. Perhaps that was why Billings was so fond of her.

"I much prefer cricket," she said blandly. "A more civilized game." She handed Brooke the glass.

"Can you see Claire sitting in the bleachers?" Brooke demanded. "Surrounded by screaming, sweaty fans, watching a bunch of grown men swing at a little ball and run around in circles?"

"If I'm not mistaken," Billings said slowly, "there's a bit more to it than that."

"Sure, RBIs and ERAs and putouts and shutouts." Brooke heaved a long breath. "What the hell is a squeeze play?"

"I'm sure I have no idea."

"Doesn't matter." Brooke shrugged and gulped down some Perrier. "Claire has it in her head that watching this guy in action will give me some inspiration." She ran a fingertip down a shocking-orange ginger jar. "What I really need is a meal."

"You can get a hot dog and some beer in the park," Claire announced from the doorway.

Glancing up, Brooke gave a hoot of laughter. Claire was immaculately dressed in buff-colored linen slacks and tailored print blouse with low alligator pumps. "You're going to a ball game," Brooke reminded her, "not a museum. And I hate beer."

"A pity." Opening her alligator bag, Claire checked the contents before snapping it shut again. "Let's be on our way, then, we don't want to miss anything. Good night, Billings."

Gulping down the rest of her drink, Brooke bolted to her feet and raced after Claire. "Let's stop to eat on the way," she suggested. "It's not like missing the first act of the opera, and I had to skip lunch." She tried her forlorn orphan's look. "You know how cranky I get if I miss a meal."

"We're going to have to start putting you in front of

the camera, Brooke; you're getting better all the time."
With a slight frown at the low-slung Datsun, Claire
maneuvered herself inside. She also knew Brooke's
obsession with regular meals sprang from her lean
adolescence. "Two hot dogs," she suggested, wisely
buckling her seat belt. "It takes forty-five minutes to get
to the stadium." Claire fluffed her silver-frosted brunette
hair. "That means you should get us there in about
twenty-five."

Brooke swore and rammed the car into first. In just
over thirty minutes, she was hunting for a parking space
outside of Kings Stadium. ". . . and the kid got it
perfect on the first take," Brooke continued blithely,
swerving around cars with a bullfighter's determination.
"The two adult actors messed up, and the table collapsed
so that it took fourteen takes, but the kid had it cold
every time." She gave a loud war whoop as she spotted
an empty space, swung into it, barely nosing out another
car, then stopped with a jaw-snapping jerk. "I want you
to take a look at the film before it's edited."

"What have you got in mind?" With some difficulty,
Claire climbed out of the door, squeezing herself between the Datsun and the car parked inches beside it.

"You're casting for that TV movie, *Family in De-
cline*." Brooke slammed her door then leaned over the
hood. "I don't think you're going to want to look any
further for the part of Buddy. The kid's good, really,
really good."

"I'll take a look."

Together, they followed the crowd swarming toward
the stadium. There was a scent of heated asphalt, heavy
air and damp humanity—Los Angeles in August. Above
them the sky was darkening so that the stadium lights

sent up a white misty glow. Inside, they walked past the stands that hawked pennants and pictures and programs. Brooke could smell popcorn and grilled meat, the tang of beer. Her stomach responded accordingly.

"Do you know where you're going?" she demanded.

"I always know where I'm going," Claire replied, turning into an aisle that sloped downward.

They emerged to find the stadium bright as daylight and crammed with bodies. There was the continual buzz of thousands of voices over piped-in, soft-rock music. Walking vendors carried trays of food and drink strapped over their shoulders. Excitement. Brooke could feel the electricity of it coming in waves. Instantly, her own apathy vanished to be replaced by an avid curiosity. People were her obsession, and here they were, thousands of them, packed together in a circle around a field of green grass and brown dirt.

Something other than hunger began to stir in her.

"Look at them all, Claire," she murmured. "Is it always like this, I wonder."

"The Kings are having a winning season. They're leading their division by three games, have two potential twenty-game-winning pitchers and a third baseman who's batting three seventy-eight for the year." She sent Brooke a lifted-brow look. "I told you to do your homework."

"Mm-hmm." But Brooke was too caught up in the people. Who were they? Where did they come from? Where did they go after the game was over?

There were two old men, perched on chairs, their hands between their knees as they argued over the game that hadn't yet started. Oh, for a cameraman, Brooke thought, spotting a five-year-old in a Kings fielder's cap

gazing up at the two gnarled fans. She followed Claire
down the steps slowly, letting her eyes record everything. She liked the size of it, the noise, the smell of
damp, crowded bodies, the color. Navy-blue-and-white
Kings pennants were waved; children crammed pink
cotton candy into their mouths. A teenager was making a
play for a cute little blonde in front of him who pretended
she wasn't interested.

Abruptly Brooke stopped, dropping her hand on
Claire's shoulder. "Isn't that Brighton Boyd?"

Claire glanced to the left to see the Oscar-winning
actor munching peanuts from a white paper bag. "Yes.
Let's see now, this is our box." She scooted in, then
lifted a friendly hand to the actor before she sat. "This
should do very well," Claire observed with a satisfied
nod. "We're quite close to third base here."

Still looking at everything at once, Brooke dropped
into her chair. The Colosseum in Rome, she thought,
must have had the same feel before the gladiators
trooped out. If she were to do a commercial on baseball,
it wouldn't be of the game, but of the crowd. A pan, with
the sound low—then gradually increase it as the camera
closed in. Then, *bamm!* Full volume, full effect. Clichéd
or not, it was quintessentially American.

"Here you go, dear." Claire disrupted her thoughts
by handing her a hot dog. "My treat."

"Thanks." After taking a healthy bite, Brooke continued with her mouth full. "Who does the advertising for
the team, Claire?"

"Just concentrate on third base," Claire advised as
she sipped at a beer.

"Yes, but—" The crowd roared as the home team
took the field. Brooke watched the men move to their

positions, dressed in dazzling white with navy-blue caps and baseball socks. They didn't look foolish, she mused as the fans continued to cheer. They looked rather heroic. She focused on the man on third.

Parks's back was to her as he kicked up a bit of dust around the base. But Brooke didn't strain to see his face. At the moment, she didn't need it—his build was enough. Six one, she estimated, a bit surprised by his height. No more than a hundred and sixty pounds—but not thin. She leaned her elbows on the rail, resting her chin on her hands.

He's lanky, she thought. He'll show off clothes well. Parks dipped for a grounder then returned it to short. For an instant, Brooke's thoughts scattered. Something intruded on her professional survey that she quickly brushed aside. The way he moved, she thought, Catlike? No. She shook her head. No, he was all man.

She waited, unconsciously holding her breath as he fielded another grounder. He moved loosely, apparently effortlessly, but she sensed a tight control as he stepped, bent, pivoted. It was a fluid action—feet, legs, hips, arm. A dancer had the same sort of nonchalant perfection after practicing a basic routine for years. If she could keep him moving, Brooke mused, it wouldn't matter if the man couldn't say his own name on camera.

There was an unexpected sexuality in every gesture. It was there even when he stood, idly waiting to field another practice ball. It might just work after all, Brooke reflected as her eyes roamed up his body, brushing over the blond curls that sprang around the sides and back of his cap. It might just . . .

Then he turned. Brooke found herself staring full into his face. It was long and lean like his body, a bit

reminiscent of the gladiators she'd been thinking about
earlier. Because he was concentrating, his full, passionate mouth was unsmiling; the eyes, almost the same
shade as the navy hat that shaded them, were brooding.
He looked fierce, almost warlike, definitely dangerous.
Whatever Brooke had been expecting, it hadn't been this
tough, uncompromisingly sexy face or her own reaction
to it.

Someone called out to him from the stands. Abruptly,
he grinned, transforming into a friendly, approachable
man with an aura of easy charm. Brooke's muscles
relaxed.

"What do you think of him?"

A bit dazed, Brooke leaned back in her chair and
absently munched on her hot dog. "He might work,"
she murmured. "He moves well."

"From what I've been told," Claire said dryly, "you
haven't seen anything yet."

As usual, Claire was right. In the first inning, Parks
made a diving catch along the base line at third for the
final out. He batted fourth, lining a long single to left
field that he stretched into a double. He played, Brooke
thought, with the enthusiasm of a kid and the diabolical
determination of a veteran. She didn't have to know
anything about the game to know the combination was
unstoppable.

In motion, he was a pleasure to watch. Relaxed now,
the first staggering impression behind her, Brooke began
to consider the angles. If his voice were as good as the
rest of him, she mused. Well . . . that was yet to be
seen. After polishing off another hot dog, she resumed
her position leaning against the rail. The Kings were

ahead 2–1 in the fifth inning. The crowd was frantic. Brooke decided she would use some action shots of Parks in slow motion.

It was hot and still on the diamond. A fitful breeze fluttered the flag and cooled the spectators high up in the stands, but below, under the lights, the air was thick. Parks felt the sweat run down his back as he stood on the infield grass. Hernandez, the pitcher, was falling behind on the batter. Parks knew Rathers to be a power hitter who pulled to the left. He planted himself behind the bag and waited. He saw the pitch—a waist-high fast ball—heard the crack of the bat. In that one millisecond, he had two choices: catch the ball that was lined hard at him or end up with a hole in his chest. He caught it, and felt the vibration of power sing through his body before he heard the screams of the crowd.

A routine catch, most would say. Parks was surprised the ball hadn't carried him out of the stadium. "Got any leather left on your glove?" the shortstop called to him as they headed back to the dugout. Parks shot him a grin before he let his eyes drift up to the stands. His eyes locked on Brooke's, surprising them both.

In reaction, Parks slowed a bit. Now there was a face, he thought, a man wouldn't see every day. She looked a bit like a ravished eighteenth-century aristocrat with her wild mane of hair and English rose skin. He felt an immediate tightening in his stomach. The face exuded cool, forbidden sex. But the eyes . . . His never left them as he approached the dugout. The eyes were soft-gray and direct as an arrow. She stared back at him without a blink or a blush, not smiling as most fans would do if they were bold, or looking away if they were shy. She just stared, Parks thought, as if she were dissecting him. With simultaneous twinges of annoyance and curiosity, he stepped into the dugout.

He thought about her as he sat on the bench. Here, the atmosphere was subdued and tense. Every game was important now if they were to maintain their lead and win the division pennant. Parks had the personal pressure of having a shot at a four hundred batting average for the year. It was something he struggled not to think about and was constantly reminded of by the press. He watched the leadoff batter ground out and thought of the redhead in the box behind third base.

Why had she looked at him like that? As if she wondered how he would look on a trophy case. With a soft oath, Parks rose and put on his batting helmet. He'd better get his mind off the little number in the stands and on the game. Hernandez was slowing down, and the Kings needed some insurance runs.

The second batter bounced one to shallow right and beat out the ball. Parks went to stand on deck. He stretched his arms over his head, one hand on the grip, the other on the barrel. He felt loose and warm and ready. Irresistibly, his eyes were drawn to his left. He couldn't see Brooke clearly from this distance, but he sensed she watched him still. Fresh annoyance broke through him. When the batter flied out, Parks approached the box.

What was her problem, anyway? he demanded as he took a testing swing. It would have been simpler if he could have characterized her as a typical Baseball Annie, but there was nothing typical about that face—or about those eyes. Planting his feet, he crouched into position and waited for the pitch. It came in high and sweet. Parks took a cut at it just before the ball dropped.

Coolly, he stepped out of the box and adjusted his helmet before he took his batting stance again. The next ball missed the corner and evened the count. Patience was the core of Parks's talent. He could wait, even when the pressure was on, for the pitch he wanted. So he waited, taking another ball and an inside strike. The crowd was screaming, begging for a hit, but he concentrated on the pitcher.

The ball came at him at ninety miles an hour, but he had it judged. This was the one he wanted. Parks swung, getting the meat of the bat on the ball. He knew it was gone the moment he heard the crack. So did the pitcher, who watched his two-strike pitch sail out of the park.

Parks jogged around the bases while the crowd roared. He acknowledged the slap of the first base coach with a quick grin. He'd never lost his childlike pleasure in hitting the long ball. As he rounded second, he automatically looked over at Brooke. She was sitting, chin on the rail, while the crowd jumped and screamed around her. There was the same quiet intensity in her eyes—no light of congratulations, no pleasure. Irritated, Parks tried to outstare her as he rounded third. Her eyes never faltered as he turned for home. He crossed the plate, exhilarated by the homer and furious with an unknown woman.

"Isn't that marvelous?" Claire beamed over at Brooke. "That's his thirty-sixth home run this season. A very talented young man." She signaled a roving concessionaire for another drink. "He was staring at you."

"Mm-hmm." Brooke wasn't willing to admit that her pulse rate had soared with each eye contact. She knew his type—good-looking, successful and heartless. She met them every day. "He'll look good on camera."

Claire laughed with the comfortable pleasure of a woman approaching fifty. "He'd look good anywhere."

Brooke's answer was a shrug as the game went into its seventh inning. She paid no attention to the score or to the other players as she watched Parks steadily. She remained, arms over the rail, chin on hands, booted feet crossed. There was something about him, she mused, something beyond the obvious attraction, the basic sexuality. It was that looseness of movement overlying the discipline. That's what she wanted to capture. The combination would do more than sell de Marco's clothes, it would typify them. All she had to do was guide Parks Jones through the steps.

She'd have him swinging a bat in immaculately sophisticated sports clothes—maybe riding through the surf in de Marco jeans. Athletic shots—that's what he was built for. And if she could get any humor out of him, something with women. She didn't want the usual adoring stares or knowing looks, but something fanciful and funny. If the script writers could pull it off and Jones could take any sort of direction. Refusing to look at the ifs, Brooke told herself she would make it work. Within the year, every woman would want Parks Jones and every man would envy him.

The ball was hit high and was curving foul. Parks chased after it, racing all the way to the seats before it dropped into the crowd four rows back. Brooke found herself face-to-face with him, close enough to smell the faint muskiness of his sweat and to see it run down the side of his face. Their eyes met again, but she didn't move, partly because she was interested, partly because she was paralyzed. The only thing that showed in her eyes was mild curiosity. Behind them there were shouts of triumph as someone snagged the foul as a trophy.

Enraged, Parks stared back at her. "Your name?" he demanded in undertones.

He had that fierce, dangerous look on his face again. Brooke schooled her voice to calmness. "Brooke."

"All of it, damn it," Parks muttered, pressed for time and furious with himself. He watched one thin eyebrow lift and found himself wanting to yank her out of the stands.

"Gordon," Brooke told him smoothly. "Is the game over?"

Parks narrowed his eyes before he moved away. Brooke heard him speak softly. "It's just beginning."

Chapter 2

BROOKE HAD BEEN EXPECTING THE CALL—AFTER ALL, he had her name, and her name was in the book. But she hadn't been expecting it at six-fifteen on a Sunday morning.

Groggily, she groped for the phone as it shrilled, managing to grip the receiver as the cradle fell heavily to the floor. "'Lo," she mumbled without opening her eyes.

"Brooke Gordon?"

"Mmm." She snuggled back into the pillow. "Yeah."

"It's Parks Jones."

Instantly alert, Brooke opened her eyes. The light was soft and dim with dawn, early birds just beginning to chirp. She fumbled for the dented windup alarm beside her bed, then scowled at the time. Biting back a torrent of abuse, she kept her voice soft and sulky. "Who?"

Parks shifted the receiver to his other hand and scowled. "Parks Jones, third base. The Kings game the other night."

Brooke yawned, taking her time about fluffing up her pillow. "Oh," was all she said, but a smile flashed wickedly.

"Look, I want to see you. We're flying back after the game in New York this afternoon. How about a late dinner?" Why was he doing this? he asked himself as he paced the small hotel room. And why, in God's name, wasn't he doing it with a bit more style?

"Dinner," Brooke repeated languidly while her mind worked fast. Wasn't it just like his type to expect a woman to have no plans that couldn't be altered to suit him? Her first instinct was to give him a cold refusal, then her sense of the ridiculous got the better of her. "Well . . ." She drew out the word. "Maybe. What time?"

"I'll pick you up at nine," Parks told her, ignoring the maybe. When he couldn't get a woman out of his head for three days, he was going to find out why. "I've got the address."

"All right, Sparks, nine o'clock."

"Parks," he corrected tersely and broke the connection.

Falling back on the pillow, Brooke started to laugh.

She was still in high good humor when she dressed that evening. Still, she thought it was too bad that the file she had read on Parks hadn't contained a bit more than all those baseball statistics. A few personal details would have given her more of an edge. What would Parks Jones have to say if he knew he was taking his future director to dinner? she wondered. Somehow Brooke didn't think he'd be too pleased when he learned she'd left out that little piece of information. But the whole scenario was too good to miss. And there was the fact that he'd touched off something in her that she wanted to get out of her system before they started to work together.

Wrapped in a bath towel, Brooke pondered her wardrobe. She didn't date often—her choice. Early experience had influenced her attitude toward men. If they were good-looking and charming, Brooke steered clear of them.

She'd been only seventeen when she'd met her first good-looking charmer. He'd been twenty-two and fresh out of college. When he'd come into the diner where she had worked, Clark had been quick with a joke and generous with a tip. It had started with a late movie once or twice a week, then an afternoon picnic in the park. It hadn't bothered Brooke that he wasn't working. He'd told her he was taking the summer off before he settled down to a job.

His family was well connected, genteel and Bostonian. The genteel, Clark had explained with an acerbic humor that had fascinated her, meant there were plenty of heirlooms and little ready cash. They had plans for him that he was consistently vague about with the carelessness of the young. He'd mentioned his family now and again—grandparents, sisters—with a humor that spoke of an intimacy she envied almost painfully. Clark could make fun of them, Brooke realized, because he *was* one of them.

He'd needed a bit of freedom, he'd claimed, a few months to flow after the regimentation of college. He wanted to be in touch with the *real* world before he chose the perfect career.

Young and starved for affection, Brooke had soaked up everything he'd told her, believed every line. He had dazzled her with an education she had wished for but had never been able to have. He'd told her she was beautiful and sweet, then had kissed her as though he meant it. There had been afternoons at the beach with rented surfboards she'd hardly noticed that she'd paid for. And when she'd given him her innocence in a kind of panicked, shamed excitement, he had seemed pleased with her. He'd laughed at her naive embarrassments and had been gentle. Brooke had thought she'd never been happier.

When he'd suggested they live together, she'd agreed eagerly, wanting to cook and clean for him, longing to wake and sleep with him. The fact that her meager salary and tips now supported both of them had never crossed her mind. Clark had talked of marriage the same way he had talked of his work—vaguely. They were something for the future, something practical that people in love shouldn't dwell on. Brooke had agreed, rosily happy with what she'd thought was her first real home. One day they would have children, she had thought. Boys with Clark's handsome face, girls with his huge brown eyes. Children with grandparents in Boston who would always know who their parents were and where their home was.

For three months she'd worked like a Trojan, setting aside part of her small salary for the future Clark always talked of while he pursued what he called his studies and systematically rejected all the jobs in the want ads as unsuitable. Brooke could only agree. To her, Clark was much too smart for any manual labor, much too important for any ordinary position. When the right job came along, she knew he would simply stride into it then zoom to the top.

At times he'd seemed restless, moody. Because she had always had to steal her own privacy, Brooke had left him to his. And when he snapped out of it, he'd always been bursting with energy and plans. Let's go here, let's go there. Now, today. Tomorrow was always years away to Clark. To Brooke, for the first time in seventeen years, today was special. She had something—*someone*—who belonged to her.

In the meantime, she'd worked long hours, cooked his meals and hoarded her tips in a small apothecary jar on a shelf in the kitchen.

One night Brooke had come home from a late shift to find that Clark had gone, taking with him her small black-and-white television set, her record collection and her apothecary jar. A note was in its place.

Brooke,

Got a call from home. My parents are putting on the pressure—I didn't know it would start so soon. I should have told you before, but I guess I kept thinking it would just go away. An old family tradition—a merger with my third cousin, as in matrimony. Hell, it sounds archaic, but it's the way my people work. Shelley's a nice girl, her dad's a connection of my dad's. I've been more or less engaged to her for a couple of years, but she was still at Smith, so it didn't seem important. Anyway, I'll slip into her family's business. Junior executive with a shot at the V.P. in five years or so. I guess I hoped I'd tell them to take a leap when the time came, but I can't. I'm sorry.

There's no fighting a wall of family and old money and stiff New England practicality, babe, especially when they keep reminding you that you're the heir apparent. I want you to know that these last couple of months I've had more breathing space than I've had in a long time, and I suppose than I'll have in an even longer time.

I'm sorry about the TV and stuff, but I didn't have the cash for the plane fare and the time wasn't right to tell my folks I'd already blown my savings. I'll pay you back as soon as I can.

I kept hoping it wouldn't have to be this way, but I'm backed into a corner. You've been great, Brooke, really great. Be happy.

Clark

Brooke had read the note twice before all the words registered. He'd gone. Her things hadn't mattered but he had. Clark was gone and she was alone—again—because she hadn't graduated from Smith or had a family in Boston or a father who could offer someone she loved a comfortable job so he'd choose her. No one had ever chosen her.

Brooke had wept until she was drained, unable to believe that her dreams, her trust and her future had been destroyed all in one instant.

Then she had grown up fast, pushing her idealism behind her. She wasn't going to be used ever again. She wasn't going to compete ever again with women who had all the advantages. And she wasn't going to slave in a steamy little diner for enough money to keep herself in a one-room apartment with dingy paint.

She had torn the note into tiny pieces, then had

washed her face with icy water until all the traces of all
the tears were gone.

Walking the pavement with all the money she had left
in her pocket, she had found herself in front of Thorton
Productions. She had gone in aggressively, belligerent-
ly, talking her way past the receptionist and into the
personnel office. She'd come out with a new job, making
hardly more than she had waiting tables, but with fresh
ambition. She was going places. The one thing her
betrayal by Clark had taught her was that she could
depend on only one person: herself. No one was ever
going to make her believe, or make her cry again.

Ten years later, Brooke drew a narrow black dress
from her closet. It was a severely sophisticated outfit she
had bought mainly for the cocktail circuit that went hand
in hand with her profession. She fingered the silk, then
nodded. It should do very well for her evening with
Parks Jones.

As Parks drove through the hills above L.A. he
considered his actions. For the first time in his career he
had allowed a woman to distract him during a game—
and this one hadn't even tried. For the first time, he had
called a virtual stranger from three thousand miles away
to make a date, and she didn't even know who the hell he
was. For the first time, he was planning on taking out a
woman who made him absolutely furious without having
said more than a handful of words. And if it hadn't been
for the road series that had followed that night game at
Kings Stadium, he would have called her before this.
He'd looked up her number at the airport on his way to
catch a plane to New York.

He downshifted for the incline as he swung around a

curve. All during the flight home, he had thought of Brooke Gordon, trying to pigeonhole her. A model or an actress, he had concluded. She had the face for it—not really beautiful, but certainly unique. Her voice was like something whispering through layers of smoke. And she hadn't sounded overly bright on the phone that morning, he reminded himself with a grimace as he stepped on the gas. There was no law that said brains had to go with intriguing looks, but something in her eyes that night . . . Parks shook off the feeling that he'd been studied, weighed and measured.

A rabbit darted out in front of him then stopped, hypnotized by his beams. Parks braked, swerved and swore as it raced back to the side of the road. He had a weakness for small animals that his father had never understood. Then, his father had understood little about a boy who chose to play ball rather than assume a lucrative position of power in Parkinson Chemicals.

Parks slowed to check his direction, then turned down the darkened back road that led to Brooke's tidy wooded property. He liked it instantly—the remoteness, the melodious sound of crickets. It was a small slice of country thirty-five minutes from L.A. Perhaps she wasn't so slow-witted after all. He pulled his MG behind her Datsun and looked around him.

Her grass needed trimming, but it only added to the rural charm of the house. It was a small, A-frame structure with lots of glass and a circular porch. He heard the tinkle of water from the narrow stream that ran behind the house. There was a scent of summer—hot, heavy blossoms he couldn't identify, and an inexplicable aura of peacefulness. He found himself wishing he didn't have to drive back down to a crowded restaurant and bright lights. In the distance a dog began to bark frantically, sending out echos to emphasize the openness. Parks climbed out of the car, wondering what sort of woman would choose a house so far from city comforts.

There was an old brass knocker in the shape of a hog's head at the right of the door. It made him grin as he let it bang. When she opened the door, Parks forgot all the doubts that had plagued him on his drive through the hills. This time he thought she looked like a seductive witch—fair skin against a black dress, a heavy silver amulet between her breasts. Her hair was pulled back at the temples with two combs, then left to fall wildly down to her hips. Her eyes were as misty as hell-smoke, the lids darkened by some subtle, glittering shadow. Her mouth was naked. He caught a drift of scent that brought him a picture of East Indian harems, white silk and dusky female laughter.

"Hello." Brooke extended her hand. It took every ounce of willpower to complete the casual gesture. How was she to have known her heart would start thudding at the sight of him? It was foolish, because she had already imagined what he would look like in sophisticated clothes. She'd had to if she was to plan how to film him. But somehow his body looked rangier, even more male in a suit coat and slacks—and somehow his face was even more attractive in the shadowed half-light of her front porch. Her plans to ask him in for a drink were aborted. The sooner they were in a crowd the better. "I'm starving," she said as his fingers closed over hers. "Shall we go?" Without waiting for his answer, she shut the door at her back.

Parks led her to the car then turned. In heels, she was nearly eye level with him. "Want me to put the top up?"

"No." Brooke opened the door herself. "I like the air."

She leaned back and shut her eyes as he started back down toward the city. He drove fast, but with the studied control she had sensed in him from the beginning. Since speed was one of her weaknesses, she relaxed and enjoyed.

"What were you doing at the game the other night?"

Brooke felt the smile tug at her mouth but answered smoothly. "A friend had some tickets. She thought I might find it interesting."

"Interesting?" Parks shook his head at the word. "And did you?"

"Oh, yes, though I'd expected to be bored."

"I didn't notice any particular enthusiasm in you," Parks commented, remembering her calm, direct stare. "As I recall, you didn't move through nine innings."

"I didn't need to," she returned. "You did enough of that."

Parks shot her a quick look. "Why were you staring at me?"

Brooke considered for a moment, then opted for the truth. "I was admiring your build." She turned to him with a half smile. The wind blew the hair into her face, but she didn't bother to brush it aside. "It's a very good one."

"Thanks." She saw a flash of humor in his eyes that pleased her. "Is that why you agreed to have dinner with me?"

Brooke smiled more fully. "No. I just like to eat. Why did you ask me?"

"I liked your face. And it's not every day I have a woman stare at me as if she were going to frame me and hang me on her wall."

"Really?" She gave him an innocent blink. "I'd think that pretty typical in your profession."

"Maybe." He took his eyes off the road long enough to meet hers. "But then you're not typical, are you?"

Brooke lifted a brow. Did he know he'd given her what she considered the highest compliment? "Perhaps not," she murmured. "Why don't you think so?"

"Because, Brooke Gordon, I'm not typical either." He burst out of the woods and onto the highway. Brooke decided that she'd better tred carefully.

The restaurant was Greek, with pungent foods, spicy scents and violins. While Parks poured her a second glass of ouzo, Brooke listened to a waiter in a grease-splattered apron sing lustily as he served souvlaki. As always, atmosphere pulled at her. Caught up, she watched and absorbed while managing to put away a healthy meal.

"What are you thinking?" Parks demanded. Her eyes shifted to his, disconcerting in their directness, seducing in their softness.

"That this is a happy place," she told him. "The sort you imagine a big family running. Momma and Poppa in the kitchen fussing over sauces, a pregnant daughter chopping vegetables while her husband tends bar. Uncle Stefos waits tables."

The image made him smile. "Do you come from a large family?"

Immediately the light went out of her eyes. "No."

Sensing a boundary, Parks skirted around it. "What happens when the daughter has her baby?"

"She pops it in a cradle in the corner and chops more vegetables." Brooke broke a hunk of bread in half and nibbled.

"Very efficient."

"A successful woman has to be."

Leaning back, Parks swirled his drink. "Are you a successful woman?"

"Yes."

He tilted his head, watching the candlelight play on her skin. "At what?"

Brooke sipped, enjoying the game. "At what I do. Are you a successful man?"

"At the moment." Parks flashed a grin—the one that gave his face a young, rather affable charm. "Baseball's a fickle profession. A ball takes a bad hop—a pitcher blows a few by you. You can't predict when a slump will start or stop—or worse, why."

It seemed a bit like life to her. "And do you have many?"

"One's too many." With a shrug, he set his drink back on the table. "I've had more than one."

With her first genuine curiosity, Brooke leaned forward. "What do you do to get out of one?"

"Change bats, change batting stances." He shrugged again. "Change your diet, pray. Try celibacy."

She laughed, a warm, liquid sound. "What works best?"

"A good pitch." He, too, leaned forward. "Wanna hear one?"

When her brow rose again, he lifted a finger to trace it. Brooke felt the jolt shiver down to her toes. "I think I'll pass."

"Where do you come from?" he murmured. His

fingertip drifted down over her cheek, then traced her jawline. He'd known her skin would feel like that. Milkmaid soft.

"No place in particular." Brooke reached for her glass, but his hand closed over hers.

"Everyone comes from somewhere."

"No," she disagreed. His palm was harder than she had imagined, his fingers stronger. And his touch was gentler. "Not everyone."

From her tone, Parks realized she was speaking the truth as she saw it. He brushed a thumb over her wrist, finding her pulse fast but steady. "Tell me about yourself."

"What do you want to know?"

"Everything."

Brooke laughed but spoke with perfect truth. "I don't tell anyone everything."

"What do you do?"

"About what?"

He should have been exasperated, but found himself grinning. "About a job, for starters."

"Oh, I make commercials," she said lightly, knowing he would conclude she worked in front of the cameras. The game had a certain mischievous appeal for her.

"I'll be doing that myself soon," he said with a quick grimace. "Do you like it?"

"I wouldn't do it if I didn't."

He sent her a narrowed look, then nodded. "No, you wouldn't."

"You don't sound as though you're looking forward to trying it," Brooke commented, slipping her hand from his. Prolonged contact with him, she discovered, made it difficult to concentrate, and concentration was vital to her.

"Not when I have to spout some silly lines and wear somebody else's clothes." Idly, he toyed with a lock of her hair, wrapping it around his finger while his eyes remained on hers. "You've a fascinating face; more alluring than beautiful. When I saw you in the stands, I thought you looked like a woman out of the eighteenth century. The sort who had a string of anxious lovers."

With a low sound of humor, Brooke leaned closer. "Was that the first pitch, Mr. Jones?"

Her scent seemed intensified by the warmth of the candle. He wondered that every man in the room wasn't aware of it, and of her. "No." His fingers tightened briefly, almost warningly, on her hair. "When I make my first one, you won't have to ask."

Instinctively, Brooke retreated, but her eyes remained calm, her voice smooth. "Fair enough." She would definitely put him on film with women, she decided. Sultry brunettes for contrast. "Do you ride?" she asked abruptly.

"Ride?"

"Horses."

"Yeah," he answered with a curious laugh. "Why?"

"Just wondered. What about hang gliding?"

Parks's expression became more puzzled than amused. "It's against my contract, like skiing or racing." He didn't trust the light of humor in her eyes. "Should I know what game you're playing?"

"No. Can we have dessert?" She flashed him a brilliant smile he trusted less.

"Sure." Watching her, Parks signaled the waiter.

Thirty minutes later, they walked across the parking lot to his car. "Do you always eat like that?" Parks demanded.

"Whenever I get the chance." Brooke dropped into the passenger seat then stretched her arms over her head in a lazy, unconsciously sensual movement. No one who hadn't worked in a restaurant could fully appreciate eating in one. She'd enjoyed the food . . . and the evening. Perhaps, she mused, she'd enjoyed being with Parks because they'd spent three hours together and still didn't know each other. The mystery added a touch of spice.

In a few months, they would know each other well. A director had no choice but to get to the inside of an actor—which is what Parks would be, whether he liked it or not. For now, Brooke chose to enjoy the moment, the mystery and the brief companionship of an attractive man.

When Parks sat beside her, he reached over to cup her chin in his hand. She met his eyes serenely and with that touch of humor that was beginning to frustrate him. "Are you going to let me know who you are?"

Odd, Brooke mused, that he would have the same understanding of the evening she did. "I haven't decided," she said candidly.

"I'm going to see you again."

She gave him an enigmatic smile. "Yes."

Wary of the smile, and her easy agreement, Parks started the engine.

He didn't like knowing that she was playing him . . . any more than he liked knowing he'd have to come back for more. He'd known a variety of women—from icy sophisticates to bubbly groupies. There were infinite shadings in between, but Brooke Gordon seemed to fit none of them. She had both a haughty sexuality and a soft vulnerability. Though his first instinct had been to get her to bed, he now discovered he wanted more. He wanted to peel off the layers of her character and study each one until he understood the full woman. Making love to her would only be part of the discovery.

They drove in silence while an old, soft ballad crooned on the radio. Brooke had her head thrown back, face to the stars, knowing it was the first time in months she'd fully relaxed on a date and not wanting to analyze why. Parks didn't find it necessary to break a comfortable silence with conversation, nor had he found it necessary to slip in those predictable hints about how he'd like to end the evening. She knew there wouldn't be a wrestling match on the side of the road or an embarrassing, infuriating argument when they reached her front door. He was safe, Brooke decided, and closed her eyes. It seemed things were going to work very well after all. Her thoughts began to drift toward her schedule for the next day.

The motion of the car woke her, or rather the lack of motion. Brooke opened her eyes to find the MG parked in her drive, the engine quiet. Turning her head, she saw Parks sprawled in his seat, watching her.

"You drive very well," she murmured. "I don't usually trust anyone enough to fall asleep in a car."

He'd enjoyed the moments of quiet while he'd watched her sleep. Her skin looked ethereal in the moonlight, ghostly pale with a hint of flush in her cheeks. The wind had tossed her hair so that Parks knew how it would look spread on a pillow after a wild night of loving. Sooner or later he'd see it that way, he determined. After his hands had tangled it.

"This time you're staring," Brooke pointed out.

And he smiled—not the quick grin she'd come to expect, but a slow, unsettling smile that left his eyes dark and dangerous. "I guess we'll both have to get used to it."

Leaning over, he opened her door. Brooke didn't stiffen or shift away from the brush of his body against hers; she simply watched. As if, Parks mused, she were considering his words very carefully. Good, he thought as he stepped from the car. This time she'd have something to think about.

"I like this place." He didn't touch her as they walked up the path to her house, though Brooke had expected him to take her hand or her arm. "I had a house in Malibu once."

"Not anymore?"

"Got too crowded." He shrugged as they walked up the porch steps. Their footsteps echoed into the night. "If I'm going to live out of the city, I want a place where I'm not forever stumbling over my neighbor."

"I don't have that problem here." Around them the woods were dark and quiet. There was only the bubbling sound of the stream and the music of tireless crickets. "There's a couple who live about a quarter mile that way." Brooke gestured to the east. "Newlyweds who met on a television series that folded." Leaning back against the door, she smiled. "We don't have any trouble keeping out of each other's way." She sighed, comfortably sleepy and relaxed. "Thanks for dinner." When she offered her hand, she wondered if he would take it or ignore it and kiss her. Brooke expected the latter, even wondered with a drowsy curiosity what the pressure of his lips on hers would be like.

Parks knew what she expected, and her lips, as they had from the first, tempted him. But he thought it was time this woman had something unexpected. Taking her hand, Parks leaned toward her. He saw from her eyes that she would accept his kiss with her own sultry reserve. Instead, he touched his lips to her cheek.

At the brush of his open mouth on her skin, Brooke's fingers tightened in his. Usually she viewed a kiss or embrace distantly, as from behind a camera, wondering dispassionately how it would appear on film. Now she saw nothing, but felt. Low, turbulent waves of sensation swept through her, making her tense. Something seemed to ripple along her skin, though he never touched her—just his hand over hers, just his lips on her cheek.

Slowly, watching her stunned eyes, Parks journeyed to her other cheek, moving his lips with the same feather-lightness. Brooke felt the waves rise until there was an echoing roar in her head. She heard a soft moan, unaware that it was her own. As hunger swept over her, Brooke turned her mouth toward his, but he glided up her skin, whispering over her eyelids so that they fluttered down. Drugged, she allowed him to roam over her face, leaving her lips trembling with anticipation and unfulfilled. She tasted his breath on them, felt the warm flutter as they passed close, but his mouth dropped to her chin to give her a teasing touch of his tongue.

Her fingers went limp in his. Surrender was unknown to her, so she didn't recognize it. Parks did as he caught the lobe of her ear between his teeth. His body was throbbing, aching to press against hers and feel the yielding softness that came only from woman. Against his cheek, her hair was as silky as her skin, and as fragrant. It took every ounce of control to prevent his hands from diving into it, to keep himself from plundering the mouth that waited, warm and naked, for his. He traced her ear with his tongue and felt her shudder. Slowly, he brushed kisses up her temple and over her brow on his way to her other ear. He nibbled gently, letting his tongue slide over her skin until he heard her moan again.

Still he avoided her mouth, pressing his lips to the pulse in her throat, fighting the urge to move lower, to feel, to taste the subtle sweep of her breast beneath the black silk. Her pulse was jerky, like the sound of her breathing. High up in the mountains, a coyote called to the moon.

A dizzying excitement raced through him. He could have her now—feel that long, willowy body beneath his, tangle himself in that wild mane of hair. But he wouldn't have all of her. He needed more time for that.

"Parks." His name came throatily through her lips, arousing him further. "Kiss me."

Gently, he pressed his lips to her shoulder. "I am."

Her mouth felt as though it were on fire. She had thought she understood hunger, having felt it too often in the past. But she'd never known a hunger like this. "Really kiss me."

He drew away far enough to see her eyes. There was no light in them now; they were opaque with desire. Her lips were parted in invitation, her breath shuddering through them. He bent close, but kept his lips an aching whisper from hers. "Next time," he said softly.

Turning, he left her stunned and wanting.

Chapter 3

"OKAY, LINDA, TRY TO LOOK LIKE YOU'RE ENJOYING this." Brooke cast a look at her lighting director and got a nod. "E. J., sweep up, starting at her toes—take your time on the legs."

E. J. gave her a blinding white grin from his smooth mahogany face. "My pleasure," he said affably and focused his camera on the actress's pink painted toenails.

"It's so hot," Linda complained, fussing with the strap of her tiny bikini. She was stretched out on a towel in the sand—long, blond and beautiful, with a rich golden tan that would hawk a popular suntan lotion. All Linda had to do was to look lush and lazy and purr that she had an *Eden* tan. The bikini would do the rest.

"Don't sweat," Brooke ordered. "You're supposed to be glowing, not wet. When we roll, count to six, then bring up your right knee—slow. At twelve, take a deep breath, pass your right hand through your hair. Say your line looking straight at the camera and think sex.''

"The hell with sex, I'm roasting.''

"Then let's get it in one take. All right. Speed. Roll film, and . . . action.''

E. J. moved up from the manicured toenails, up the long, slender legs, over a rounded hip, golden midriff and barely confined bosom. He closed in on Linda's face—sulky mouth, pearly teeth and baby blues—then went back for a full shot.

"I've got an *Eden* tan,'' Linda claimed.

"Cut.'' Brooke swiped a hand over her brow. Though it was still morning, the beach was baking. She thought she could feel the sand burning through the soles of her sneakers. "Let's pump a little life into it,'' she suggested. "We've got to sell this stuff on one line and your body.''

"Why don't you try it?'' Linda demanded, falling onto her back.

"Because you're getting paid to and I'm not,'' Brooke snapped, then clicked her teeth together. She knew better than to lose her temper, especially with this one. The trouble was that since her evening with Parks, she'd been on a perpetual short fuse. Taking a deep breath, Brooke reminded herself that her personal life, if that's what Parks Jones was, couldn't interfere with her work. She walked over and crouched beside the pouting model. "Linda, I know it's miserable out here today, but a job's a job. You're a pro or you wouldn't be here.''

"Do you know how hard I worked on this tan to get this lousy thirty-second spot?''

Brooke patted her shoulder, conveying sympathy,

understanding and authority all at once. "Well then, let's make it a classic."

It was past noon before they were able to load up their equipment. E. J. reached in the back of the station wagon he used and pulled two iced drinks out of a chest cooler. "Here ya go, boss."

"Thanks." Brooke pressed the cold bottle against her forehead before she twisted off the top. "What was with her today?" she demanded. "She can be a problem, but I've never had to drag one line out of her like that before."

"Broke up with her man last week," E. J. informed Brooke before he took a greedy swallow of grape soda.

Grinning, Brooke sat on the tailgate. "Anything you don't know, E. J.?"

"Not a thing." He propped himself beside her, one of the few on the Thorton staff who wasn't leery of the Tiger-Lady, as Brooke had been dubbed. "You're going to that fancy de Marco party tonight."

"Yeah." Brooke gave a slow, narrowed-eyed smile that had nothing to do with the brilliance of the sun. The party would be her chance to cut Parks Jones down a few pegs. She could still remember how she had stood shaking on her porch in the moonlight after the echo of his engine had died away.

"It's going to be a kick working with Parks Jones." E. J. downed the rest of his soda in one swallow. "The man's got the best glove in the league and a bat that won't quit smoking. Knocked in two more RBIs last night."

Brooke leaned against the door frame and scowled. "Good for him."

"Don't you like baseball?" E. J. grinned, tossing his empty bottle into the back of the wagon.

"No."

"Ought to have some team spirit," he mused and gave her knee a friendly squeeze. "The better he does, the more punch the campaign'll have. And if he gets into the series—"

"If he gets into the series," Brooke interrupted, "we have to wait until the end of October before we can start shooting."

"Well." E. J. stroked his chin. "That's show biz."

Brooke tried to glare, then chuckled. "Let's get back. I've got a shoot in the studio this afternoon. Want me to drive?"

"Naw." E. J. slammed the tailgate then headed for the driver's seat. "I like living."

"You're such a wimp, E. J."

"I know," he agreed cheerfully. "I've got this thing about traveling at the speed of light." After adjusting mirror-lensed sunglasses on his face he coaxed the station wagon's engine into life. It sputtered and groaned temperamentally while he crooned to it.

"Why don't you buy a new car?" Brooke demanded. "You get paid enough."

He patted the wagon's dash when the engine caught. "Loyalty. I've been cruising in this little darling for seven years. She'll be around when that flashy machine of yours is nuts and bolts."

Brooke shrugged, then tilted back her head to drain the bottle. E. J. was the only one who worked under her who dared any intimacy, which was probably the reason she not only allowed it but liked him for it. She also considered him one of the best men with a camera on the

the West Coast. He came from San Francisco where his father was a high school principal and his mother owned and operated a popular beauty salon. She had met them once and wondered how two such meticulous people could have produced a free-wheeling, loose-living man with a penchant for voluptuous women and B movies.

But then, Brooke mused, she'd never been able to understand families. Always she viewed them with perplexity and longing, as only one on the outside could fully understand. Settling back on the carefully patched seat, she began to plot out her strategy for her afternoon session.

"Heard you took in a Kings game the other night." E. J. caught her swift, piercing look and began to whistle tunelessly.

"So?"

"I saw Brighton Boyd at a party a couple of nights ago. Worked with him on a TV special last year. Nice guy."

Brooke remembered seeing the actor in the box next to hers and Claire's. She dropped her empty bottle on the already littered floor. "So?" she repeated coolly.

"Big Kings fan," E. J. went on, turning the radio up loud so that he had to shout over the top 40 rock. "Raved about Jones's homer—on a two-out, two-strike pitch. The man's a hell of a clutch hitter." While Brooke remained silent, E. J. tapped out the beat from the radio on the steering wheel. There was the glint of gold from a ring on his long dark fingers. "Brighton said Jones stared at you like a man who'd been hit with a blunt instrument. That Brighton, he sure does turn a phrase."

"Hmm." Brooke began to find the passing scenery fascinating.

"Said he came right over to your box chasing a foul. Had a few words to say."

Brooke turned her head and stared into E. J.'s mirrored glasses. "Are you pumping me, E. J.?"

"Hot damn! Can't pull anything over on you, Brooke; you're one sharp lady."

Despite herself she laughed. She knew a "no comment" would only cause speculation she'd like to avoid. Instead she stretched her legs out on the seat and treated it lightly. "He just wanted my name."

"And?"

"And nothing."

"Where'd you go with him?"

The faintest frown creased her brow. "I didn't say I went anywhere with him."

"He didn't ask your name because he was taking a census."

Brooke gave him a cool, haughty look that would have discouraged anyone else. "You're a gossipy old woman, E. J."

"Yep. You go to dinner with him?"

"Yes," she said on a sigh of surrender. "And that's all."

"Not as bright as he looks, then." He patted her sneakered foot. "Or maybe he felt funny about starting something up with the lady who'll be directing him."

"He didn't know," Brooke heard herself say before she could stop herself.

"Oh?"

"I didn't tell him."

"Oh." This time the syllable was drawn out and knowing.

"I didn't think it was necessary," Brooke said heatedly. "It was strictly a social meeting, and it gave me the opportunity to plan how best to film him."

"Mm-hmm."

She turned back in her seat and folded her arms. "Shut up and drive, E. J."

"Sure thing, boss."

"As far as I'm concerned he can take his golden glove and smoking bat and sit on them."

E. J. nodded wisely, enjoying himself. "You know best."

"He's conceited and cold and inconsiderate."

"Must have been some evening," E. J. observed.

"I don't want to talk about it." Brooke kicked at the empty bottle on the floor.

"Okay," he said affably.

"He's the kind of man," she went on, "who thinks a woman's just waiting to fall all over him just because he's moderately attractive and successful and has an average mind."

"For a Rhodes scholar," E. J. mused as he slowed down for his exit.

"A what?"

"He's a Rhodes scholar."

Brooke's mouth fell open, then shut with a bang. "He is not."

E. J. shrugged agreeably. "Well, that's what it said in *Sports View*. That was supposed to be the main reason he didn't start playing professional ball until he was twenty-two."

"Probably just a publicity hype," she muttered, but

she knew better. She rode the rest of the way to the studio in frowning silence.

The de Marco California villa was an eyeful. Brooke decided that it had the dubious ability of making Claire's mansion look simple and discreet. It was huge, E-shaped and dazzling white with two inner courtyards. One held a grottolike pool complete with miniature waterfall, the other a sheltered garden rich with exotic scents.

When Brooke arrived, she could hear the high liquid sounds of harps and mixed conversation. People were ranged through the house, spilling outdoors and clustered in corners. Passing through the gold-toned parlor, she caught the mingling, heady scents of expensive perfumes and spiced food. There was the glitter of diamonds, swirl of silks and flash of tanned, pampered skin.

Brooke caught snatches of conversations as she strolled through, searching for the main buffet.

"But darling, he simply can't carry a series anymore. Did you see him at Ma Maison last week?"

"She'll sign. After that fiasco in England, she's itching to come back to Hollywood."

"Can't remember a line if you feed it to him intravenously."

"Left her for the wardrobe mistress."

"My dear, have you ever seen *such* a dress!"

Hollywood, Brooke thought with halfhearted affection as she pounced on the remains of the pâté.

"I knew I'd find you here."

Brooke turned her head as she speared a chunk of smoked beef. "Hello, Claire," she managed over a mouthful of cracker. "Nice party."

"I suppose, as you always judge them by the menu." Claire gave her a long, appraising look. Brooke wore a buckskin jumpsuit, soft and smooth as cream, with a thick pewter belt cinched at her waist. She'd braided the hair at her temples and clipped it back over the flowing tousled mane, letting heavy pewter links dangle at her ears. Because she'd been distracted while applying it, she'd neglected her makeup and had only remembered to darken her eyes. As a result, they dominated her pale, sharp-featured face. "Why is it you can wear the most outlandish outfits and still look marvelous?"

Brooke grinned and swallowed. "I like yours, too," she said, noting that Claire was, as always, stylishly neat in pale-blue voile. "What have they got to drink in this place?"

With a sigh, Claire motioned to a roving, red-suited waiter and chose two tulip glasses of champagne. "Try to behave yourself. The de Marcos are very old-fashioned."

"I'll be a credit to the company," Brooke promised and lifted her hand in acknowledgment of a wave from a stand-up comic she'd directed in a car commercial. "Do you think I could get a plate?"

"Gorge later. Mr. Jones's agent is here, I want you to meet him."

"I hate talking to agents on an empty stomach. Oh, damn, there's Vera. I should have known she'd be here."

Brooke answered the icy smile from the slim honey-haired model who was the current embodiment of the American look. Their paths had crossed more than once, professionally and socially, and the women had taken an instant, lasting dislike to each other. "Keep your claws sheathed," Claire warned. "De Marco's going to be using her."

"Not with me," Brooke said instantly. "I'll take the ball player, Claire, but someone else is going to hold the leash on that one. I don't like my poison in small doses."

"We'll discuss it," Claire muttered then beamed a smile. "Lee, we were just looking for you. Lee Dutton, Brooke Gordon. She's going to be directing Parks." She placed a maternal hand on Brooke's arm. "My very best."

Brooke lifted an ironic brow. Claire was always lavish with praise in public and miserly with it behind closed doors. "Hello, Mr. Dutton."

Her hand was grabbed hard and pumped briskly. Discreetly, Brooke flexed her fingers while she made a swift survey. He was shorter than she was and rather round with thinning hair and startling black eyes. A creature of first impressions, she liked him on the spot.

"Here's to a long, successful relationship," he announced and banged his glass exuberantly against hers. "Parks is eager to begin."

"Is he?" Brooke smiled, remembering Parks's description of his venture into commercials. "We're just as eager to have him."

Claire sent her a brief warning look as she tucked her arm through Lee's. "And where is he? Brooke and I are both anxious to meet him."

"He has a hard time getting away from the ladies." Lee gave the proud, apologetic smile of a doting uncle. But the eyes on Brooke were shrewd.

"How awkward for him," she murmured into her glass. "But I suppose he manages to live with it."

"Brooke, you really must try the pâté." Claire sent her a teeth-clenched smile.

"I did," Brooke returned easily. "Tell me more about Parks, Mr. Dutton. I can't tell you what a fan I am."

"Oh, you follow baseball?"

Brooke tilted her glass again. "Why, we were in the park only a few weeks ago, weren't we, Claire?"

"As a matter of fact." Claire didn't bother to try to outstare Brooke this time but turned to Lee. "Do you get to many games?"

"Not enough," he admitted, knowing a game was afoot and willing to play. "But I happen to have a few tickets for Sunday's game," he said, making a mental note to arrange for some. "I'd love to escort both you ladies."

Before Brooke could open her mouth, Claire doled out subtle punishment. "There's nothing we'd like better."

He caught Brooke's quick scowl before she smoothed her features. "Well, there's Parks now." Lee bellowed for him, causing heads to turn before conversation buzzed again.

Parks's first reaction was surprise when he saw Brooke standing beside his agent and the woman he knew was head of Thorton Productions. Then he experienced the same flare of reluctant desire he had felt on the other two occasions he'd seen her. He'd purposely let the days pass before he contacted her again, hoping the power of need would lessen. One glance at her told him it hadn't worked.

Apparently without hurry, he weaved through the crowd, stopping to exchange a few words when someone touched his arm, then gently disentangling himself. He'd learned, at an early age, how to keep from being cornered at a social occasion. In less than two minutes, Parks stood in front of Brooke.

Well done, Brooke thought. She answered Parks's smile cautiously, wondering what his reaction would be when they were introduced. She felt a jab of uneasiness then pushed it aside. After all, he'd been the one to wake her up at dawn and ask for a date.

"Parks, I want you to meet Claire Thorton, the lady who'll be producing your commercials." Lee laid his hand over Claire's in an unconsciously possessive gesture noticed only by Parks and Brooke. Parks was amused, Brooke annoyed.

"A pleasure, Ms. Thorton." He wanted to say he had expected a dragon from what he'd read of her professionally, not this soft-faced attractive woman with faded blue eyes. Instead, Parks smiled and accepted her hand.

"We're looking forward to working with you. I was just telling Mr. Dutton how much Brooke and I enjoyed your game against the Valiants a few weeks ago." Remembering his muttered demand for Brooke's name at the rail, Claire waited for the reaction.

"Oh?" So this was her friend, he thought, turning to Brooke. With her face, he concluded she must be a regular for Thorton's commercials. "Hello again."

"Hello." Brooke found her hand claimed and held. Taking a hasty sip of champagne, she waited for the bomb to drop.

"Claire tells me Ms. Gordon is her best," Lee told Parks. "Since you'll be working together closely, you'll want to get to know each other."

"Will we?" Parks ran his thumb along Brooke's palm.

"Only my best director for a project this important," Claire put in, watching them closely.

Brooke felt his thumb stop its casual caress, then his fingers tightened. There was no change in his face. To prevent a quick gasp of pain, she swallowed the rest of her champagne. "So you direct commercials," he said smoothly.

"Yes." She tugged once to free her hand, but he only increased his grip.

"Fascinating." Casually, he plucked the empty glass from her other hand. "Excuse us." Brooke found herself being dragged through the crowd of jewels and silks. Immediately, she quickened her pace so that it appeared she was walking with him rather than being led.

"Let go of me," she hissed, giving a nodding smile to another director. "You're breaking my hand."

"Consider it a preview of things to come." Parks pulled her through the open French doors, hoping to find a quiet spot. There was a three-piece band in the garden playing soft, dancing music. At least a dozen couples were taking advantage of it. Parks swore, but before he could maneuver her through the garden to a more private spot, he heard someone call her name. Immediately, he dragged her into his arms.

The hard contact with his chest stole her breath, the arm tight around her waist prevented her from finding any more. Ignoring the choking sound she made, Parks began to sway to the music. "Just wave to him," he ordered against her ear. "I'm not about to be interrupted with small talk."

Wanting to breathe again, Brooke obeyed. She was already planning revenge. When his grip lessened slightly, she drew in a sharp breath of air, letting it out on a string of abuse. "You overgrown bully, don't think you can drag me around just because you're this year's American hero. I'll only take it once, and I'll only warn you once. Don't you *ever* grab me again." Brooke stomped hard on his foot and was rewarded by having her air cut off again.

"You dance beautifully, Ms. Gordon," Parks whispered in her ear. He bit none too gently on the lobe. Between the fury and pain, Brooke felt a stir deep in her stomach. Oh, no, she thought, stiffening. Not again. The band switched to an up-tempo number but he continued to hold her close and sway.

"You're going to have a lot of explaining to do when I faint from lack of oxygen," she managed. Who would have thought that lanky body would be so hard, or the limber arms so strong?

"You won't faint," he muttered, slowly maneuvering her toward the edge of the garden. "And you're the one with the explaining to do."

She was released abruptly, but before Brooke could take a breath, he was pulling her through a clump of azalea. "Look, you jerk . . ." Then she was back inside, dazed by bright lights and laughter. Without pausing, Parks dragged her through the center patio and into the adjoining courtyard.

There was no music here, except the liquid sound of the water falling into the grotto, and only a few couples more intent on themselves than on a man pulling a furious woman in his wake. Parks drew her close to the pool and into the shadows behind the high wall. Brooke was effectively sandwiched between him and the smooth rocks.

"So you like to play games," he murmured.

For the first time she was able to lift her face and stare into his. Her eyes glittered in the moonlight. "I don't know what you're talking about."

"No?"

She had expected him to be annoyed, but she hadn't expected this smoldering fury. It was in his eyes, in the hard lines of his face, in the poised readiness of his body. When she felt her heart begin to thud uncomfortably, she became only more defensive. "You made all the moves," she tossed out. "You *demanded* that I give you my name. You called *me* at six o'clock in the morning for a date. All I did was let Claire drag me to a ball game."

She made an attempt to push by him and found herself pressed back against the wall by a firm hand on her chest. "You were sizing me up," he said slowly. "At the game, at dinner. Tell me, how did I come out?"

Brooke put her hand to his wrist, but was surprised when he let her push his hand away. She began a careless recital she knew would infuriate him. "You move more like a dancer than an athlete—it'll be a plus on film. Your build is good, it'll sell clothes. You can be charming at times, and your face is attractive without being handsome. That could sell anything. You have a certain sexuality that should appeal to women who'd like their men to have it, too. They're the primary target, as women still do the bulk of buying in ready-to-wear."

Her tone had been schooled to annoy. Even so, Parks couldn't prevent his temper from rising. "Do I get a rating?"

"Naturally." The bitten-off words pleased her enormously. It was a small payment for the scene on her porch, but it was payment. "Your popularity quotient is fair at the moment. It should get higher after the first commercial is aired. Claire seems to think if you could get into the World Series and do something outstanding, it would help."

"I'll see what I can do," he said dryly. "Now, why didn't you tell me who you were?"

"I did."

He leaned closer. She caught a trace of sharp cologne over the smell of wet summer leaves. "No, you didn't."

"I told you I make commercials."

"Knowing I'd conclude you were an actress."

"Your conclusions are your own problem," Brooke told him with a shrug. "I never said I was an actress." She heard a woman's laugh muffled in the distance and the rush of water into the pool beside her. The odds, she mused, were not in her favor at the moment. "I don't see what difference it makes."

"I don't like games," Parks said precisely, "unless I know the players."

"Then we won't play," Brooke countered. "Your job is to do what I tell you—no more, no less."

Parks controlled a wave of fury and nodded. "On the set." He caught the hair at her waist, then let it slide through his hands. "And off?"

"And off, nothing." She'd put more emphasis on the last word than she had intended to. It showed a weakness she could only hope he didn't notice.

"No." Parks stepped closer so that she had to tilt back her head to keep her eyes level with his. "I don't think I like those rules. Let's try mine."

Brooke was ready this time for the sneak attack on her senses. He wouldn't be permitted to seduce her, make her tremble with those feather-light teasing kisses on her skin. With a cool, hard stare, she dared him to try.

He returned the look as seconds dragged on. She caught the glint of challenge in his eyes but didn't see the slow curve of his lips. No man had ever been able to meet her stare so directly or for so long. For the first time in years, Brooke felt a weakness in her primary defense.

Then he did what he had wanted to do from the first moment he had seen her. Parks dove his hands into the lushness of her hair, letting them sink into the softness before he dragged her against him. Their eyes clashed a moment longer, even as he lowered his lips and savaged hers.

Brooke's vision blurred. She struggled to bring it back into sharp focus, to concentrate on that one sense to prevent her others from being overpowered. She fought not to taste the hot, demanding flavor of his lips, to feel the quick, almost brutal nip of his teeth that would tempt her lips to part. She didn't want to hear her own helpless moan. Then his tongue was plundering, enticing hers to answer in a seduction totally different from the teasing gentleness of his first embrace. She struggled against him, but her movements only caused more heat to flare from the friction of her body on his.

Gradually, the kiss altered. The hard pressure became sweet. He nibbled at her mouth, as if savoring the flavor, sucking gently, though his arms kept her pinned tight. She lost even her blurred vision, and her will to resist went with it.

Parks felt the change, her sudden pliancy. Her surrender excited him. She wasn't a woman to relinquish control easily, yet both times he had held her, he'd prized it from her. With gentleness, he realized, suddenly aware that the anger had fled from his body and his mouth. It was gentleness that won her, whereas force would only be met with force. Now he didn't want to think—not for a moment. He wanted only to lose himself in the soft give of her body, the white-silk scent that poured from her and the dusky flavor of her mouth. They were all the seduction of woman, only intensified by her surrender.

Brooke felt the liquid weight in her limbs, the slow insistent tug in her thighs before the muscles went lax. Her mouth clung to his, yearning for more of the magic it could bring with the gentle play of tongue and teeth. His hands began a slow exploration of her body, kneading over the soft material. When she felt him loosen the narrow zipper that ran from her throat to her waist, she roused herself to protest.

"No." The words came on a gasp of breath as his fingers slid along her skin.

Parks gathered her hair in one hand, drawing her head back so that his eyes met hers again. "I have to touch you." Watching her, he glided his fingers over her breast, pausing briefly on the taut point before he roamed down to her flat, quivering stomach. "One day I'll touch all of you," he murmured. "Inch by inch. I'm going to feel your skin heat under my hands." His fingers trailed back to her breast, leaving a path of awakened flesh in their wake. "I'm going to watch your face when I make love to you."

Bending, he touched his lips to hers again, tasting her breath as it shuddered into his mouth. Very slowly, he drew up the zipper, letting his knuckles graze along her skin. Then he ran his hands up her back until their bodies fit together again.

"Kiss me, Brooke." He rubbed his nose lightly against hers. "Really kiss me."

Tingling from his touch, aroused by the whispered words, she pressed her open mouth to his. Her tongue sought his, hungry for the moist dark tastes that had already seeped inside of her. He waited for her demands, her aggressions, feeling them build as her body strained against his. With a groan of pleasure, Brooke tangled her fingers in his hair, wanting to drag him closer. When he knew his chain of control was on its last link, Parks drew her away. He'd learned more of her, but not enough. Not yet. And he wasn't going to forget that he had a small score to settle with her.

"When the camera's rolling, it's your game and your rules." He cupped her chin in his hand, wondering how many times he'd be able to walk away from her when his body was aching to have her. "When it's not," he continued quietly, "the rules are mine."

Brooke took a shaky breath. "I don't play games."

Parks smiled, running a fingertip over her swollen mouth. "Everyone does," he corrected. "Some make a career out of it, and they aren't all on ball fields." Dropping his hand, he stepped back from her. "We both have a job to do. Maybe we're not too thrilled about it at the moment, but I have a feeling that won't make any difference in how well you work."

"No," Brooke agreed shortly. "It won't. I can detest you and still make you look fantastic on the screen."

He grinned. "Or make me look like an idiot if it suited you."

She couldn't prevent a small smile from forming. "You're very perceptive."

"But you won't, because you're a pro. Whatever

happens between us personally won't make you direct any differently.''

''I'll do my job,'' Brooke stated as she stepped around him. ''And nothing's going to happen between us personally.'' She looked up sharply when a friendly arm was dropped over her shoulder.

''I guess we'll just wait and see about that.'' Parks sent her another amiable grin. ''Have you eaten?''

Brooke frowned at him dubiously. ''No.''

He gave her shoulder a fraternal pat. ''I'll get you a plate.''

Chapter 4

BROOKE COULDN'T BELIEVE SHE WAS SPENDING A PER-
fectly beautiful Sunday afternoon at a ball game. What
was more peculiar was that she was enjoying it. She was
well aware that she was being punished for the few
veiled sarcastic remarks she had tossed off at the de
Marco party, but after the first few innings, she found
that Billings was right. There was a bit more to it than
swinging a bat and running around in circles.

During her first game, Brooke had been too caught up
in the atmosphere, the people, then in her initial impressions of Parks. Now she opened her mind to the game
itself and enjoyed. Being a survivor, whenever she was
faced with doing something she didn't want to do,
Brooke simply conditioned herself to *want* to do it. She
had no patience with people who allowed themselves to
be miserable when it was so simple to turn a situation

around to your advantage. If it wasn't always possible to enjoy, she could learn. It pleased her to be doing both.

The game had more subtlety than she had first realized, and more strategy. Brooke never ceased to be intrigued by strategy. It became obvious that there were variables to the contest, dozens of ifs, slices of chance counterbalancing skill. In a game of inches, luck couldn't be overlooked. This had an appeal for her because she had always considered luck every bit as vital as talent in winning, no matter what the game.

And there were certain aspects of the afternoon, beyond the balls and strikes, that fanned her interest.

The crowd was no less enthusiastic or vocal than it had been on her first visit to Kings Stadium. If anything, Brooke reflected, the people were more enthusiastic— even slightly wild. She wondered if their chants and screams and whistles took on a tone of delirium because the score was tied 1–1, and had been since the first inning. Lee called it an example of a superior defensive game.

Lee Dutton was another aspect of the afternoon that intrigued her. He seemed—on the surface—a genial, rather unkempt sort of man with a faint Brooklyn accent that lingered from his youth. He wore a golf shirt and checked pants, which only accented his tubbiness. Brooke might have passed him off as a cute middle-aged man had it not been for the sharp black eyes. She liked him . . . with a minor reservation—he seemed inordinately attentive to Claire.

It occurred to Brooke that he found a great many occasions to touch—Claire's soft manicured hands, her round shoulder, even her gabardine-clad knee. What was more intriguing to Brooke was that Claire didn't, as was her habit, freeze Lee's tentative advances with an icy smile or a stingingly polite word. As far as Brooke could tell, Claire seemed to be enjoying them—or perhaps she was overlooking them because of the importance of the de Marco account and Parks Jones. In either case, Brooke determined to keep an eye on her friend, and the agent. It wasn't unheard-of for a woman approaching fifty to be naive of men and therefore susceptible.

If she were to be truthful, Brooke would have to admit she enjoyed watching Parks. There was no doubt he was in his element in the field, eyes shaded by a cap, glove in his hand. Just as he had been in his element, she remembered, at the glossy party at the de Marco villa. He hadn't seemed out of place in the midst of ostentatious wealth, sipping vintage champagne or handling cocktail party conversation. And why should he? she mused. After their last encounter, Brooke had made it her business to find out more about him.

He'd come from money. Big money. Parkinson Chemicals was a third-generation, multimillion-dollar conglomerate that dealt in everything from aspirin to rocket fuel. He'd been born with a silver spoon in one hand and a fat portfolio in the other. His two sisters had married well, one to a restauranteur who had been her business partner before he became her husband, the other to a vice president of Parkinson attached to the Dallas branch. But the heir to Parkinson, the man who carried the old family name in front of the less unique Jones, had had a love affair with baseball.

The love affair hadn't diminished during his studies at Oxford under a Rhodes scholarship; it had simply been postponed. When Parks had graduated, he'd gone straight to the Kings' training camp—Brooke had to wonder how his family had felt about that—and there had been drafted. After less than a year on the Kings' farm team, he'd been brought up to the majors. There he had remained, for a decade.

So he didn't play for the money, Brooke mused, but because he enjoyed the game. Perhaps that was why he played with such style and steadiness.

She remembered, too, her impressions of him at the de Marcos'—charming, then ruthless, then casually friendly. And none of it, Brooke concluded, was an act. Above all else, Parks Jones was in complete control, on or off the diamond. Brooke respected that, related to it, while she couldn't help wondering how the two of them would juggle their need to be in charge when they began to work together. If nothing else, she mused as she crunched down on a piece of ice, it would be an interesting association.

Brooke watched him now as he stood on the bag at second while the opposing team brought out a relief pitcher. Parks had started off the seventh inning with a leadoff single, then had advanced to second when the next batter walked. Brooke could feel the adrenaline of the crowd pulsing while Parks talked idly with the second baseman.

"If they take this one," Lee was saying, "the Kings lock up the division." He slipped his hand over Claire's. "We need these runs."

"Why did they change pitchers?" Brooke demanded. She thought of how furious she would be if someone pulled her off a job before it was finished.

"There's two on and nobody out." Lee gave her an easy paternal smile. "Mitchell was slowing down—he'd walked two last inning and was only saved from having runs score by that rifle shot the center fielder sent home.'' Reaching in his shirt pocket, he brought out a cigar in a thin protective tube. ''I think you'll see the Kings going to the bullpen in the eighth.''

''I wouldn't switch cameramen in the middle of a shoot,'' Brooke mumbled.

''You would if he couldn't focus the lens anymore,'' Lee countered, grinning at her.

With a laugh, Brooke dove her hand into the bag of peanuts he offered her. ''Yeah, I guess I would.''

The strategy proved successful, as the relief man shut down the next three batters, leaving Parks and his teammate stranded on base. The crowd groaned, swore at the umpire and berated the batters.

''Now there's sportsmanship,'' Brooke observed, casting a look over her shoulder when someone called the batter, who struck out to end the inning, a bum—and other less kind names.

Lee gave a snort of laughter as he draped his arm casually over Claire's shoulders. ''You should hear them when we're losing, kid.''

The lifted-brow look Brooke gave Claire at the gesture was returned blandly. ''Enthusiasm comes in all forms,'' Claire observed. With a smile for Lee, she settled back against his arm to watch the top of the next inning.

Definitely an odd couple, Brooke mused; then she assumed her habitual position of elbows on rail. Parks didn't glance her way. He had only once—at the beginning of the game when he took the field. The look had been long and direct before he had turned away, and since then it was as though he wasn't even aware of her. She hated to admit it irked her, hated to admit that she would have liked to engage in that silent battle of eye to eye. He was the first man she *wanted* to spar with, though she had sparred with many since her first naive encounter ten years before. There was something exciting in the mind game, particularly since Parks had a mind she both envied and admired.

Lee was on target, as the Kings went to the bullpen when the starting pitcher walked two with one man out. Brooke shifted closer to the edge of her seat to watch Parks during the transition. What does he think about out there? she wondered.

God, what I wouldn't give for a cold shower and a gallon of beer, Parks thought as the sun beat down on the back of his neck. He'd been expecting the change of pitchers and was pleased with the choice. Ripley did well what a reliever was there to do—throw hard and fast. He gave a seemingly idle glance toward the runner at second. That could be trouble, he reflected, doing a quick mental recall of his opponent's statistics. The ability to retain and call out facts had always come naturally to Parks. And not just batting averages and stolen bases. Basically, he only forgot what he wanted to forget. The rest was stockpiled, waiting until he needed it. The trick had alternately fascinated and infuriated his family and friends, so that he generally kept it to himself. At the moment, he could remember Ripley's earned-run average, his win-loss ratio, the batting average of the man waiting to step into the batter's box and the scent of Brooke's perfume.

He hadn't forgotten that she was sitting a few yards away. The awareness of her kindled inside of him—a not quite pleasant sensation. It was more of an insistent pressure, like the heat of the sun on the back of his neck. It was another reason he longed for a cool shower. Watching Ripley throw his warm-up pitches to the catcher, Parks allowed himself to imagine what it would be like to undress her—slowly—in the daylight, just before her body went from limp surrender to throbbing excitement. Soon, he promised himself; then he forced Brooke to the back of his mind as the batter stepped up to the plate.

Ripley blew the first one by the batter—hard and straight. Parks knew that Ripley didn't throw any fancy pitches, just the fast ball and the curve. He was either going to overpower the hitters, or with the lineup of right-handers coming up, Parks was going to be very busy. He positioned himself another step back on the grass, going by instinct. He noted the base runner had a fat lead as the batter chipped the next pitch off. The runner was nearly at third before the foul was called. Ripley looked back over his shoulder at second, slid his eyes to first, then fired the next pitch.

It was hit hard, smashing into the dirt in front of third then bouncing high. There was never any opportunity to think, only to act. Parks leaped, just managing to snag the ball. The runner was coming into third in a headfirst slide. Parks didn't have the time to admire his guts before he tagged the base seconds before the runner's hand grabbed it. He heard the third base ump bellow, "Out!" as he vaulted over the runner and fired the ball at the first baseman.

While the crowd went into a frenzy, Brooke remained seated and watching. She didn't even notice that Lee had given Claire a resounding, exuberant kiss. The double play had taken only seconds—that impressed her. It also disconcerted her to discover that her pulse was racing. If she closed her eyes, she could still hear the cheers from the fans, smell the scent of sun-warmed beer and see, in slow motion, the strong, sweeping moves of Parks's body. She didn't need an instant replay to visualize the leap and stretch, the shifting of muscle. She knew a ball player had to be agile and quick, but how many of them had that dancerlike grace? Brooke caught herself making a mental note to bring a camera to the next game, then realized she had already decided to come back again. Was it Parks, she brooded, or baseball that was luring her back?

"He's something, isn't he?" Lee leaned over Claire to give Brooke a slap on the back.

"Something," Brooke murmured. She turned her head enough to look at him. "Was that a routine play?"

Lee snorted. "If you've got ice water for blood."

"Does he?"

As he drew on a cigar, Lee seemed to consider it. He gave Brooke a long, steady look. "On the field," he stated with a nod. "Parks is one of the most controlled, disciplined men I know. Of course"—the look broke with his quick smile—"I handle a lot of actors."

"Bless them," Claire said and crossed her short, slim legs. "I believe we all agree that we hope Parks takes to this, ah, alternate career with as much energy as he shows in his baseball."

"If he has ten percent of this skill"—Brooke gestured toward the field—"in front of the camera, I'll be able to work with him."

"I think you'll be surprised," Lee commented dryly, "at just what Parks is capable of."

With a shrug, Brooke leaned on the rail again. "We'll see if he can take direction."

Brooke waited, with the tension of the crowd seeping into her, as the game went into the bottom of the ninth inning. Still tied 1–1, neither team seemed able to break through the defensive skill of the other. It should have been boring, she mused, even tedious. But she was on the edge of her seat and her pulse was still humming. She wanted them to win. With a kind of guilty surprise, Brooke caught herself just before she shouted at the plate umpire for calling strike three on the leadoff batter. It's just the atmosphere, she told herself with a frown. She'd always been a sucker for atmosphere. But when the second batter came up, she found herself gripping the rail, willing him to get a hit.

"This might go into extra innings," Lee commented.

"There's only one out," Brooke snapped, not bothering to turn around. She didn't see the quick grin Lee cast at Claire.

On a three-and-two pitch, the batter hit a bloop single to center. Around Brooke, the fans went berserk. He might have hit a home run from the way they're reacting, she thought, trying to ignore the fast pumping of her own blood. This time Brooke said nothing as the pitcher was pulled. How do they stand the tension? she wondered, watching the apparently relaxed players as the new relief warmed up. Base runners talked idly with the opposition. She thought that if she were in competition, she wouldn't be so friendly with the enemy.

The crowd settled down to a hum that became a communal shout with every pitch thrown. The batter hit one deep, so deep Brooke was amazed at the speed with which the right fielder returned it to the infield.

The batter was content with a single, but the base runner had eaten up the distance to third with the kind of gritty speed Brooke admired.

Now the crowd didn't quiet, but kept up a continual howl that echoed and reverberated as Parks came to bat. The pressure, Brooke thought, must be almost unbearable. Yet nothing showed in his face but that dangerous kind of concentration she'd seen once or twice before. She swallowed, aware that her heart was hammering in her throat. Ridiculous, she told herself once, then surrendered.

"Come on, damn it," she muttered, "smack one out of here."

He took the first pitch, a slow curve that just missed the corner. The breath that she'd been holding trembled out. The next he cut at, fouling it back hard against the window of the press box. Brooke clamped down on her bottom lip and mentally uttered a stream of curses. Parks coolly held up a hand for time, then bent to tie his shoe. The stadium echoed with his name. As if deaf to the yells, he stepped back into the box to take up his stance.

He hit it high and deep. Brooke was certain it was a repeat of his performance in her first game, then she saw the ball begin to drop just short of the fence.

"He's going to tag up. He'll tag up!" she heard Lee shouting as the center fielder caught Parks's fly at the warning track. Before Brooke could swear, the fans were shouting, not in fury but in delight. The moment the runner crossed the plate, players from the Kings' dugout swarmed out on the field.

"But Parks is out," Brooke said indignantly.

"The sacrifice fly scored the run," Lee explained.

Brooke gave him a haughty look. "I realize that"—

only because she had crammed a few basic rules into her head—"but it hardly seems fair that Parks is out."

Chuckling, Lee patted her head. "He earned another RBI and the fleeting gratitude of a stadium full of Kings fans. He was one for three today, so his average won't suffer much."

"Brooke doesn't think much of rules," Claire put in, rising.

"Because they're usually made up by people who don't have the least idea what they're doing." A little annoyed with herself for becoming so involved, she stood, swinging her canvas bag over her shoulder.

"I don't know if Parks would agree with you," Lee told her. "He's lived by the rules for most of his life. Gets to be a habit."

"To each his own," she said casually. She wondered if Lee was aware that Parks was also a man who could seduce and half undress a woman behind the fragile covering of a rock wall in the middle of a crowded, glitzy Hollywood party. It seemed to her Parks was more a man who made up his own rules.

"Why don't we go down to the locker room and congratulate him?" Genially, he hooked his arms through Claire's and Brooke's, steamrolling them through the still cheering crowd.

Lee worked his way into the stadium's inner sanctum with a combination of panache and clout. Reporters were swarming, carrying microphones, cameras or notepads. Each one was badgering or flattering a sweaty athlete in the attempt to get a quote. In the closed-in area, Brooke considered the noise level to be every bit as high as it had been in the open stadium. Lockers slammed, shouts reverberated, laughter flowed in a kind of giddy relief.

Each man knew the tension would return soon enough during the play-offs. They were going to enjoy the victory of the moment to its fullest.

"Yeah, if I hadn't saved Biggs from an error in the seventh inning," the first baseman told a reporter, deadpan, "it might have been a whole different ball game."

Biggs, the shortstop, retaliated by heaving a damp towel at his teammate. "Snyder can't catch a ball unless it drops into his mitt. The rest of us make him look good."

"I've saved Parks from fifty-three errors this season," Snyder went on blandly, drawing the sweaty towel from his face. "Guess his arm must be going. Thing is, some of the hitters are so good they just keep smacking the ball right into Parks's mitt. If you watch the replay of today's game, you'll see what fantastic aim they have." Someone dumped a bucket of water on his head, but Snyder continued without breaking rhythm. "You might notice how well I place the ball in the right fielder's mitt. That takes more practice."

Brooks spotted Parks, surrounded by reporters. His uniform was filthy, streaked with dirt, while his face fared little better. The smudges of black under his eyes gave him a slightly wicked look. Without the cap his hair curled freely, darkened with sweat. But his face and body were relaxed. A smile lingered on his lips as he spoke. That battlefield intensity was gone from his eyes, she noted, as if it had never existed. If she hadn't seen it, hadn't experienced it from him, Brooke would have sworn the man wasn't capable of any form of ruthlessness. Yet he was, she reminded herself, and it wouldn't be smart to forget it.

"With only four games left in the regular season," Parks stated, "I'll be satisfied to end up with a three eighty-seven average for the year."

"If you bat five hundred in those last games—"

Parks shot the reporter a mild grin. "We'll have to see about that."

"A little wind out there today and that game-winning sacrifice fly would've been a game-winning home run."

"That's the breaks."

"What was the pitch?"

"Inside curve," he responded easily. "A little high."

"Were you trying for a four-bagger, Parks?"

He grinned again, his expression altering only slightly when he spotted Brooke. "With one out and runners on the corners, I just wanted to keep the ball off the ground. Anything deep, and Kinjinsky scores . . . unless he wants the Lead Foot Award."

"Lead Foot Award?"

"Ask Snyder," Parks suggested. "He's the current holder." With another smile, Parks effectively eased himself away. "Lee." He nodded to his agent while running a casual finger down Brooke's arm. She felt the shock waves race through her, and only barely managed not to jerk away. "Ms. Thorton. Nice to see you again." His only greeting to Brooke was a slow smile as he caught the tip of her hair between his thumb and forefinger. She thought again it was wise to remember he wasn't as safe as he appeared.

"Hell of a game, Parks," Lee announced. "You gave us an entertaining afternoon."

"We aim to please," he murmured, still looking at Brooke.

"Claire and I are going out to dinner. Perhaps you and Brooke would like to join us?"

Before Brooke could register surprise at Claire having a date with Lee Dutton, or formulate an excuse against making it a foursome, Parks spoke up. "Sorry, Brooke and I have plans."

Turning her head, she shot Parks a narrowed look. "I don't recall our making any plans."

Smiling, he gave her a brief tug. "You'll have to learn to write things down. Why don't you just wait in your box? I'll be out in half an hour." Without giving her a chance to protest, Parks strolled off toward the showers.

"What incredible nerve," Brooke grumbled, only to be given a sharp but discreet elbow in the ribs by Claire.

"Sorry you can't join us, dear," she said sweetly. "But then you're not fond of Chinese food in any case. And Lee's going to show me his collection first."

"Collection?" Brooke repeated blankly as she was steered into the narrow corridor.

"We've a mutual passion." Claire gave Lee a quick and surprisingly flirtatious smile. "For Oriental art. Can you find your way back to the seats?"

"I'm not a complete dolt," Brooke muttered, while giving Lee a sceptical stare.

"Well then." Casually, Claire tucked her hand into Lee's beefy arm. "I'll see you Monday."

"Have a good time, kid," Lee called over his shoulder as Claire propelled him away.

"Thanks a lot." Stuffing her hands in her pockets, Brooke worked her way up, then out to the lower level, third-base box. "Thanks a hell of a lot," she repeated and stared out at the empty diamond.

There were a few maintenance workers scooping up the debris in the stands with humming heavy-duty cleaners, but other than that the huge open area was deserted. Finding it strangely appealing, Brooke discovered her annoyance waning. An hour before, the air had been alive, throbbing with the pulse of thousands. Now it was serene, with only the faintest trace of the crowd—the lingering odor of humanity, a whiff of salted popcorn, a few discarded cardboard containers. She leaned back against the rail, more interested in the empty stadium than the empty field.

When had it been built? she wondered. How many generations had crammed themselves into the seats and aisles to watch the games? How many thousands of gallons of beer had traveled along the rows of seats? She laughed a little, amused by her own whimsy. When a player stopped playing, did he come here to watch and remember? She thought Parks would. The game, she concluded, would get into your blood. Even she hadn't been immune to it . . . or, she thought wryly, to him.

Brooke tossed her head back, letting her hair fall behind her. The shadows were lengthening, but the heat still had the sticky, sweltering capacity of high afternoon. She didn't mind—she hated being cold. Habitually, she narrowed her eyes and let herself visualize how she would approach the stadium on film. Empty, she thought, with the echo of cheers, the sound of a ball cracking off a bat, a banner left behind to flutter in the breeze. She'd use the maintenance workers, sucking up the boxes and cups and bags. She might title it *Afterthought,* and there'd be no telling if the home team had left the field vanquished or victorious. What mattered would be the perpetuity of the game, the people who played it and the people who watched.

Brooke sensed him before she heard him—only an instant, but the instant was enough to scatter her thoughts and to bring her eyes swerving toward him. Immediately, all sense of the scene she had been setting vanished from her mind. No one else had ever had the power to do that to her. The fact that Parks did baffled her nearly as much as it infuriated her. For Brooke, her work was the one stability in her life—nothing and no one was allowed to tamper with it. Defensively, she straightened, meeting his stare head-on as he walked down to her in the loose, rangy stride that masked over a decade of training.

She expected him to greet her with some smart remark. Brooke was prepared for that. She considered he might greet her casually, as if his lie in the locker room had been perfect truth. She was prepared for that, too.

She wasn't prepared for him to walk directly to her, bury his hands in her hair and crush her against him in a long, hotly possessive kiss. Searing flashes of pleasure rocketed through her. Molten waves of desire overpowered surprise before it truly had time to register. His mouth pressed against hers in an absolute command that barely hid a trace of desperation. It was that desperation, more than the authority, that Brooke found herself responding to. The need to be needed was strong in her—she had always considered it her greatest weakness. And she was weak now, with the sharp scent of his skin in her senses, the dark taste of his mouth on her tongue, the feel of his shower-damp hair on her fingers.

Slowly, Parks drew her away, waiting for her heavy

lids to lift. Though his eyes never left hers, Brooke felt as though he looked at all of her once, thoroughly. "I want you." He said it calmly, though the fierce look was back on his face.

"I know."

Parks ran a hand through her hair again, from the crown to the tips. "I'm going to have you."

Steadying a bit, Brooke stepped out of his arms. "That I don't know."

Smiling, Parks continued to caress her hair. "Don't you?"

"No," Brooke returned with such firmness that Parks lifted a brow.

"Well," he considered, "I suppose it could be a very pleasant experience to convince you."

Brooke tossed her head to free her hair of his seeking fingers. "Why did you lie to Lee about our having plans tonight?"

"Because I'd spent nine long, hot innings thinking about making love to you."

Again he said it calmly, with just a hint of a smile on his lips, but Brooke realized he was quite serious. "Well, that's direct and to the point."

"You prefer things that way, don't you?"

"Yes," she agreed, settling back against the rail again. "So let me do the same for you. We're going to be working together for several months on a very big project that involves a number of people. I'm very good at my job and I intend to see that you're very good at yours."

"So?"

Her eyes flashed at his amused tone, but Brooke continued. "So personal involvements interfere with professional judgment. As your director, I have no intention of becoming your lover, however briefly."

"Briefly?" Parks repeated, studying her. "Do you always anticipate the length of your relationships before-hand? I think," he continued slowly, "you're more of a romantic than that."

"I don't care what you think," she snapped, "as long as you understand."

"I understand," Parks agreed, beginning to. "You're evading the issue."

"I certainly am not!" Temper flared, reflecting in her stance and her eyes as well as her voice. "I'm telling you straight out that I'm not interested. If that bruises your ego, too bad."

Parks grabbed her arm when she would have swept by him. "You know," he began in a careful tone that warned of simmering anger, "you infuriate me. I can't remember the last time a woman affected me that way."

"I'm not surprised." Brooke jerked her arm out of his hold. "You've been too busy devastating them with your charm."

"And you're too worried about being dumped to have any kind of a relationship."

She made a quick, involuntary sound, as if she'd been struck. Cheeks pale, eyes dark, she stared at him before she shoved him aside to race up the stairs. Parks caught her before she'd made it halfway. Though he turned her back to face him firmly, his touch was gentle.

"Raw nerve?" he murmured, feeling both sympathy and guilt. It wasn't often he lost control enough to say something he'd have to apologize for. Eyes dry and hurting, Brooke glared at him. "I'm sorry."

"Just let me go."

"Brooke." He wanted to pull her into his arms and comfort, but knew she wouldn't accept it. "I am sorry. I don't make a habit of punching women."

It wasn't charm, but sincerity. After a moment, Brooke let out a long breath. "All right. I usually take a punch better than that."

"Can we take off the gloves—at least for the rest of the day?" How deep was the hurt? Parks wondered. And how long would it take to win her trust?

"Maybe," Brooke returned cautiously.

"How about dinner?"

She responded to the smile before she realized it. "My weakness."

"We'll start there, then. How do you feel about tacos?"

She allowed him to take her hand. "Who's buying?"

They sat outdoors at a busy fast-food franchise with tiny metal tables and hard stools. Sounds of traffic and blaring car radios rolled over them. Brooke relaxed when she ate, Parks noted, wondering if she were consciously aware of the dropping of guards. He didn't think so. The relaxation was the same when she sat in an elegant restaurant with wine and exotic food as it was in a greasy little take-out with sloppy tacos and watered-down sodas in paper cups. After handing her another napkin, Parks decided to do some casual probing.

"Did you grow up in California?"

"No." Brooke drew more soda through her straw. "You did."

"More or less." Remembering how skilled she was in evading or changing the subject, Parks persisted. "Why did you move to L.A.?"

"It's warm," she said immediately. "It's crowded."

"But you live miles out of town in the middle of nowhere."

"I like my privacy. How did your family feel about you choosing baseball over Parkinson Chemicals?"

He smiled a little, enjoying the battle for control. "Stunned. Though I'd told them for years what I intended to do. My father thought, still thinks, it's a phase. What does your family think about you directing commercials?"

Brooke set down her cup. "I don't have any family."

Something in her tone warned him this was a tender area. "Where did you grow up?"

"Here and there." Quickly, she began to stuff used napkins into the empty cups. Parks caught her hand before she could rise.

"Foster homes?"

Eyes darkening with anger, Brooke stared at him. "Why are you pressing?"

"Because I want to know who you are," he said softly. "We could be friends before we're lovers."

"Let go of my hand."

Instead of obliging, Parks gave her a curious look. "Do I make you nervous?"

"You make me furious," she tossed back, evading one truth with another. "I can't be around you for more than ten minutes without getting mad."

Parks grinned. "I know the feeling. Still, it's stimulating."

"I don't want to be stimulated," Brooke said evenly. "I want to be comfortable."

With a half laugh, Parks turned her hand over, brushing his lips lightly over the palm. "I don't think so," he murmured, watching her reaction over their joined hands. "You're much too alive to settle for comfortable."

"You don't know me."

"Exactly my point." He leaned a bit closer. "Who are you?"

"What I've made myself."

Parks nodded. "I see a strong, independent woman with lots of drive and ambition. I also see a woman who chooses a quiet, isolated spot for her home, who knows how to laugh and mean it, who forgives just as quickly as she angers." As he spoke Parks watched her brows lower. She wasn't angry now, but thoughtful and wary. He felt a bit like a man trying to gain the confidence of a dove who might fly away at any time or choose to nestle in the palm of his hand. "She interests me."

After a moment, Brooke let out a long breath. Perhaps if she told him a little, she considered, he'd leave it at that. "My mother wasn't married," she began briskly. "I'm told that after six months she got tired of lugging a baby around and dumped me on her sister. I don't remember a great deal about my aunt, I was six when she turned me over to social services. What I do remember is being hungry and not very warm. I went into my first foster home." She shrugged then pushed away the debris that littered the table. "It wasn't too bad. I was there for a little more than a year before I got shuffled to the next one. I was in five altogether from the age of six to seventeen. Some were better than others, but I never belonged. A lot of that may have been my fault."

Brooke sighed, not pleased to remember. "Not all foster parents take in children for the money. Some of them—most of them," she amended, "are very kind, loving people. I just never felt a part, because I always knew it would be temporary, that my sister or brother of the moment was real and I was . . . transient. As a result I was difficult. Maybe I challenged the people whose home I was placed in to want me—for me, not out of pity or social obligation or the extra dollars my living with them would bring in.

"My last two years in high school I lived on a farm in Ohio with a nice couple who had an angelic son who would yank my hair when his mother's back was turned." A quick grimace. "I left as soon as I graduated from high school, worked my way cross-country waiting tables. It only took me four months to get to L.A." She met Parks's quiet, steady look and suddenly flared. "Don't feel sorry for me."

The ultimate insult, he mused, taking her rigid hand in his. "I wasn't. I was wondering how many people would have the guts to try to make their own life at seventeen, and how many would have the strength to really do it. At the same age I wanted to head for the Florida training camps. Instead I was on a plane heading for college."

"Because you had an obligation," Brooke countered.

"I didn't. If I had had the chance to go to college . . ." She trailed off. "In any case, we've both had a decade in our careers."

"And you can have several more if you like," Parks pointed out. "I can't. One more season."

"Why?" she demanded. "You'll only be . . ."

"Thirty-five," he finished with a wry smile. "I promised myself ten years ago that's when I'd stop. There aren't many of us who can play past forty like Mays."

"Yes, it's obvious you play like an old man," she returned dryly.

"I intend to stop before I do."

Taking a straw, she began to pleat it while she studied him. "Quit while you're ahead?"

"That's the idea."

That she could understand. "Does giving it up with half your life ahead of you bother you?"

"I intend to do something with the second half, but at times it does. Other times I think about all those summer evenings I'll have free. Do you like the beach?"

"I don't get there often, but yes." She thought about the long, hot commercial she'd just filmed. "With occasional exceptions," she added.

"I have a place on Maui." Unexpectedly he leaned over, caressing her cheek with fingers that were whisper soft and undeniably possessive. "I'm going to take you there one day." He shook his head as Brooke started to speak. "Don't argue, we do that too much. Let's go for a drive."

"Parks," Brooke began as they rose, "I meant what I said about not getting involved."

"Yeah, I know." Then he kissed her long and lingeringly while she stood with her hands filled with paper plates and cups.

Chapter 5

IT WAS THREE DAYS BEFORE BROOKE HEARD FROM Parks. She was aware that the last four-game series in the regular season would be played out of town. She knew, too, from what she told herself was simply a casual glimpse at the sports section, that Parks had knocked in three more RBIs in the first two games. In the meantime, she was busy looking over the story board for his first block of commercials.

The word had come down that the first thirty-second spot would be filmed before the league play-offs, in order to capitalize on Parks's exposure in the competition. That left Brooke little time to prepare, with an already demanding schedule of studio and location shoots, editing and preproduction meetings. But challenge, like food, was vital to her.

Closed off in her office, with a half an hour's leeway,

before she was due at the studio, Brooke ran over the final script for the initial de Marco commercial. Casually slick, she thought, approving. It had minimal dialogue and soft sell—Parks at the plate, swinging away while dressed in de Marco's elegant sports clothes, then a slow dissolve to the next scene with him dressed in the same suit, stepping out of a Rolls with a slinky brunette on her arm.

"Clothes for anytime—anywhere," Brooke muttered. The timing had been checked and rechecked. The audio, except for Parks's one-line voice-over, was already being recorded. All she had to do was to guide Parks through the paces. The salesmanship hinged on her skill and his charm. Fair enough, she thought and reached for her half cup of cold coffee as a knock sounded at her door. "Yeah?" Brooke turned the script back to page one, running through the camera angles.

"Delivery for you, Brooke." The receptionist dropped a long white florist's box on her cluttered desk. "Jenkins said to let you know the Lardner job's been edited. You might want to check it out."

"Okay, thanks." Curiously, Brooke frowned over the top of the script at the flower box. Occasionally, she received a grateful phone call or letter from a client when they were particularly pleased with a commercial—but not flowers. Then there'd been that actor in the car spot last year, Brooke remembered. The one who was on his third wife. He'd alternately amused and annoyed Brooke by sending her batches of red roses every week. But six months had passed since she had convinced him that he was wasting her time and his money.

More likely it was one of E. J.'s practical jokes, she

considered. She'd probably find a few dozen frog legs inside. Not one to spoil someone's fun, Brooke pulled off the ribbon and lifted the lid.

There were masses of hibiscus. Fragrant, dew-soft pink-and-white petals filled the box almost to overflowing. After the first gasp of surprise, Brooke dove her hands into them, captivated by their purely feminine scent and feel. Her office suddenly smelled like a tropical island: heady, exotic, richly romantic. With a sound of pleasure, she filled her hands with the blooms, bringing them up to her face to inhale. In contrast to the sultry scent, the petals seemed impossibly fragile. A small white card fluttered down to her littered desk.

Letting the flowers drift back into the box, Brooke reached for the envelope and tore it open.

I thought of your skin.

There was nothing else, but she knew. She shuddered, then chided herself for acting like a mooning teenager. But she read the line three times. No one had ever been able to affect her so deeply with such simplicity. Though Parks was a thousand miles away, she could all but feel those lean, strong fingers trace down her cheek. The flood of warmth, the flash of desire told her she wasn't going to escape him—had never truly wanted to. Without giving herself any time for doubts or fears, Brooke picked up the phone.

"Get me Parks Jones," she said quickly. "Try Lee Dutton, he'll have the number." Before she could change her mind, Brooke hung up, burying her hands in the flowers again.

How was it he knew just what buttons to push? she

wondered, then discovered at that moment she didn't care. It was enough to be romanced—and romanced in style. Lifting a single bloom, she trailed it down her cheek. It was smooth and moist against her skin—as Parks's first kiss had been. The ringing phone caught her dreaming.

"Yes?"

"Parks Jones on line two. You've got ten minutes before they need you in the studio."

"All right. Hunt me up a vase and some water, will you?" She glanced at the box again. "Make that two vases." Still standing with the blossom in her hand, Brooke punched the button for line two. "Parks?"

"Yes. Hello, Brooke."

"Thank you."

"You're welcome."

She hesitated, then let herself speak her first thought. "I feel like a teenager who just got her first corsage."

Dropping flat on his back on the bed, he laughed. "I'd like to see you with some of them in your hair."

Experimentally she held one up over her ear. Unprofessional, she thought with a sigh, and contented herself with the scent of them. "I've a shoot in the studio in a few minutes; I don't think the lights would do them much good."

"You have your practical side, don't you, Brooke?" Parks flexed the slight ache in his shoulder and closed his eyes.

"It's necessary," she muttered but couldn't quite bring herself to drop the blossom back in the box. "How are you? I wasn't sure you'd be in."

"I got in about half an hour ago. They cut us down five to two. I went oh for three."

"Oh." She frowned, not quite sure what she was supposed to say. "I'm sorry."

"I didn't seem to have any rhythm—it'll pass." Before the play-offs, he added silently. "I thought of you, maybe too much."

Brooke felt an odd twist of pleasure that was difficult to pass off. "I wouldn't want to be responsible for a slump, particularly when I remember some of the remedies." His chuckle sounded faint and weary. "Are you tired?"

"A bit. You'd think with the division wrapped up we'd glide through this last series. Last night we went eleven innings."

"I know." She could have bitten off her tongue. "I caught the highlights on the late news," she said breezily. "I'll let you sleep, then. I just wanted to thank you."

Her inadvertent admission had his lips twitching, but he didn't bother to open his eyes. With them closed, he had no trouble bringing her face into focus. "Will I see you when I get back?"

"Of course. We'll be shooting the first segment on Friday, so—"

"Brooke," he interrupted firmly, quietly. "Will I see you when I get back?"

She hesitated, then looked down at the mass of pink-and-white hibiscus on her desk. "Yes," she heard herself saying. Pressing the flower to her cheek, she sighed. "I think I'm going to make a very big mistake."

"Good. I'll see you Friday."

The trick to being a good director, Brooke had always thought, was to be precise without being too technical, brisk without losing sympathy, then to split yourself up into several small parts so that you could be everywhere at once. It was a knack she had developed early on—on the job—without the formalized training of many of her colleagues. Perhaps because she had worked so many of the other aspects of filming, from timing a script to setting the lights to mixing sound, she was fiercely precise. Nothing escaped her eye. Because she knew actors were often overworked and insecure, she had never quite lost her sympathy for them even when she was ready to rage at a consistently flubbed line. Her early experience at waiting tables had taught her the trick of moving fast enough to all but be two places at once.

On a set or in a studio, she had complete self-confidence. Her control was usually unquestioned because it came naturally. She never thought about being in charge or felt the need to remind others of it; she simply *was* in charge.

With a copy of the script in one hand, she supervised the final adjustments on the lights and reflectors. The ball diamond, she had noted immediately, had an entirely different feel at home plate than it had from the stands. It was like being on an island, cupped amid the high mountain of seats, with the tall green wall skirting the back. The distance from plate to fence seemed even more formidable from this perspective. Brooke wondered how men with sticks in their hands could continually hit a moving ball over that last obstacle.

She could smell the grass, freshly trimmed, the dusty scent of dirt that had dried in the sun and a whiff of E. J.'s blatantly macho cologne. "Give me a reading," she ordered the lighting director as she glanced up at the thick clouds in the sky. "I want a sunny afternoon."

"You got it." The lights were focused as Brooke stepped behind camera one to check for shadows on the plate.

Parks loitered at the tunnel entrance a moment, watching her. This was a different woman from the one he had treated to tacos—different still from the one he had held in his arms at the de Marco party. Her hair was trained back in one long braid, nothing like the flowing, gypsylike mane he was used to seeing. She wore jeans that were white at the stress points, a plain T-shirt the color of scrambled eggs, dusty tennis shoes and winking sapphires at her ears.

But it wasn't her hairstyle or the apparel that denoted the difference. It was the assurance. He'd seen it before, but each time it had been underlying. Now she sparked with it, gesturing, ordering while men and women set about giving her exactly what she demanded. No one questioned her. And, he considered, it was patently obvious that she wouldn't have permitted it.

Grimacing, he tugged at the sleeve of the thin silk shirt he wore. Who the hell would play ball in an outfit like this? he wondered with a glance at the creaseless cream slacks. The rules of this game were hers, he reminded himself, then stepped into the light.

"Bigelow, get these cables secure before somebody breaks a leg. Libby, see if you can scrounge up some ice water, we're going to need it. Okay, where's . . ." Turning at that moment, Brooke spotted Parks. "Oh, there you are." If she felt any personal pleasure at seeing him, she hid it well, Parks thought wryly as she turned to shout an order at her assistant. "I'm going to want you to stand at the plate so we can check the lighting and camera angles."

Without a word, Parks complied. You might as well get used to it, he told himself. You've got yourself locked into hawking somebody else's clothes for the next two years. He stuffed his hands in his pockets, cursed Lee briefly and stood in the batter's box. Someone stuck a light meter next to his face.

"You gonna wipe out the Valiants in the play-offs?" the technician demanded.

"That's the plan," Parks returned easily.

"I've got fifty bucks on it."

This time Parks grinned. "I'll try to keep that in mind."

"Detrick." Brooke gave the technician a jerk of her head to send him on his way as she approached Parks. "Okay, this is the easy part," she began. "No dialogue, and you're doing what you're best at."

"What's that?"

Brooke lifted a brow at the loaded question but continued smoothly. "Swinging a bat. Since the pitching coach has agreed to throw you a few, you should feel comfortable."

"Ever stood in the box without a helmet?" he countered.

"It wouldn't go with your outfit," she said mildly. She gave him a deliberately slow study—eyes sweeping up, then down, then back up again. "And it looks good."

"I like yours, too." His smile was quick and dangerous. "I'm going to like unbinding your hair."

"Makeup!" she called abruptly. "Give him a dusting, he's going to glow."

"Wait a minute," Parks began, deftly catching the wrist of the woman with the powder.

"No sweating on camera," Brooke drawled, pleased with his reaction. "All I want you to do is what you usually do when you're in uniform. Take your regular stance," she continued. "A couple of those test swings. After you hit the ball, I want one of those grins before you toss the bat aside."

"What grins?" Reluctantly, Parks released the make-up artist's wrist and suffered the powder.

With humor dancing in her eyes, Brooke gave him a singularly sweet smile. "One of those boy-on-the-beach grins. Quick, lots of teeth, crinkles at the corners of the eyes."

He narrowed them dangerously. "I'm going to get you for this."

"Try to keep the strikes to a minimum," she went on blithely. "Every strike's a take. You don't have to hit it out of the park, just *look* like you have. Got it?"

"Yeah, I got it." Annoyed, he nodded to the pitching coach as he walked by.

"You look real cute, Jones."

"Just try to get it near the plate," Parks retorted. "Do I get a bat?" he demanded of Brooke. "Or do I just pretend?"

For an answer, Brooke turned and shouted to her assistant. "Let's have the bat. E. J., are you set? Just roll the film—no sweeps, no pans, no close-ups. Remember, we're selling the clothes."

"This is aluminum."

Distracted, Brooke turned back to Parks. "What?"

"This bat is aluminum."

When he held it out, Brooke automatically took it from him. "Yes, it appears to be." As she started to pass it back to him, Parks shook his head.

"I use wood. A two seventy-seven A."

She started to come back with a curt remark, then stopped herself. If she was accustomed to anything, it was temperament. "Get Mr. Jones the bat he prefers," she told her assistant, tossing the first one to him. "Anything else?"

For a moment, he regarded her keenly. "Does everybody jump when you say?"

"Damn right. Keep that in mind for the next couple of hours, and we shouldn't have any problems."

His look sharpened fractionally. "While the cameras are on," he returned in a voice only she could hear.

Turning, she walked to stand behind the camera. Automatically, E. J. stepped back so that she could check the angle herself. Brows drawn together, Brooke stared at Parks through the lens as her assistant handed him another bat. "Okay, Parks, would you take your stance?" Her frown deepened as he leaned slightly over the plate, feet planted, knees bent, shoulders lined toward the mound. The frown vanished. "Good," she decided, moving back so that E. J. could take her place.

"Ten bucks says he pulls one to left center."

A brief nod was Brooke's acceptance of the bet. "Parks, when I say action, I want you to take your stance again, then those testing swings. Keep your eye on the mound—*don't* look at the camera. Just forget we're here." With the first smile Parks had seen that morning, Brooke turned to the pitching coach. "Are you all set, Mr. Friedman?"

"All set, sweetheart. I'll try not to blow it by you, Jones."

Parks gave a snort of laughter. "Just see if you can

make it to the plate.'' He gestured to his uncovered head.
''And keep it low.''

Brooke took a last glance around, assuring herself
everyone was in position. ''Let's do one for time. Set?''
She held up her hand, waiting for absolute silence. ''Roll
film, and . . . action.''

She watched Parks crouch into position, then take two
loose swings. The deep-blue silk of his shirt caught the
light, accenting the play of muscles beneath. Hands on
her hips, Brooke counted off the seconds and waited.
Parks shifted his weight as the ball came toward him,
tensed his muscles then checked his swing. The ball
smashed into the pads behind him.

Just barely, Brooke controlled the need to swear.
''Cut.'' Battling her annoyance, she walked to him. ''Is
there a problem, Parks?''

''Pitch was outside.''

''Like hell.'' Friedman called from the mound. ''It
caught the corner.''

Immediately the crew split themselves up, arguing in
favor of the batter or the pitcher. Ignoring them for the
moment, Brooke gave her attention to Parks. ''This isn't
the bottom of the ninth, you're just supposed to hit the
ball. You'll notice,'' she continued, gesturing behind
her, ''there aren't any fielders, no fans, no press.''

Parks set the bat, barrel down in the dirt, and leaned
on the handle. ''You want me to swing at a bad pitch?''

Brooke met the amused blue eyes levelly. ''The
quality of the pitch is immaterial,'' she countered as the
argument raged behind them. ''Just hit the ball.''

With a shrug, he hefted the bat again. ''You're the
boss . . . at the moment.''

The look held, long and challenging, before Brooke

turned back to her crew. "Take two," she announced, effectively cutting off the debate.

This time Parks didn't check his swing but drilled the ball up the foul line at third. Without looking at E. J., Brooke held out her hand. "Time," she requested as a ten-dollar bill was stuffed in her palm.

Parks noticed a tiny brunette with a stop watch and clip board. "Twelve and a half seconds, Brooke."

"Good. All right, let's go for it."

"This one's going over the fence," E. J. pronounced in an undertone to Brooke. "Bet ten?"

"Take three," she called out with a nod of assent. "Roll film, and . . . action!" A satisfied smile touched her lips as she studied Parks. He was either getting into the spirit of things, or his own competitive spirit was driving him. Either way, it was working for her. The look on his face as he crouched over the plate was exactly what she wanted—the steady intensity that bordered on fierceness. A pity she couldn't work in a close-up, she mused, then lost the thought as Parks took a full swing at the pitch.

Power. The word rippled through her as he connected with the ball. She saw the instant the shirt strained over his shoulders, was aware of the bunching of muscles in his thighs beneath the soft, expensive material. It wasn't necessary to follow the path of the ball to know where it had gone. She knew the flash of grin on Parks's face had nothing to do with her direction. It was sheer pleasure. Brooke kept the film rolling as his eyes followed the ball out of the park. Still grinning, he turned to her, then gave a deprecatory shrug.

She should have been angry that he had looked at the camera against her directions, but the movement, the expression was perfect. Even as she dug in her pocket for E. J.'s ten dollars, she decided to keep it in.

"Cut."

Spontaneous applause broke out, along with a few whistles. "Nice pitch, Friedman," Parks commented.

The coach tossed another ball in the air. "Just making you look good, Jones. The Valiants' pitchers won't be so friendly."

Brooke swiped the back of her wrist across her damp brow. "I'd like a couple more please. What was the time on that?"

"Fourteen seconds."

"Okay. The light's shifting, check the reading. Mr. Friedman, I'd like to get a couple more."

"Anything you say, sweetheart."

"Parks, I need a full swing like last time. No matter where the ball goes, look up and out—don't forget the grin."

Laying the bat on his shoulder, he drawled, "No, ma'am."

Brooke ignored him and turned away. "Lights?"

The technician finished the adjustments, then nodded. "Set."

Although she considered the third take close to perfect, Brooke ran through another three. Edited, this segment of the commercial would run twelve and a half seconds. That it took only three hours to set up and film showed that she ran a tight schedule.

"It's a wrap. Thanks," she added as she accepted the cup of ice water from her assistant. "We'll set up in front of the restaurant in . . ." She glanced at her watch. "Two hours. Fred, double-check on the Rolls and the actress. E. J., I'll take the film into editing myself."

Even as she spoke, Brooke walked over to the mound. "Mr. Friedman." With a smile, she held out her hand. "Thank you."

He found her grip firm and her eyes soft. "My pleasure." With a chuckle, he tossed a spare ball into his mitt. "You know, in my day ball players plugged razor blades or beer. We endorsed bats and gloves." He cast a glance at Parks, who was signing a baseball for a technician. "No fancy designer would have asked us to sport his clothes."

Brooke shifted her eyes to Parks. He was laughing now, shaking his head at E. J. as the cameraman ticked off some point on his fingers. The casually elegant clothes suited him, as did the dark wood bat in his hand. "I'd hate to have him know I said it, Mr. Friedman," Brooke commented as she turned back to the coach, "but Parks is a natural."

With a shout of laughter, Friedman patted her on the back. "He won't hear it from me, sweetheart. Last thing my pitchers need is a third baseman with a big head. One more thing," he added before Brooke turned away. "I watched the way you run things." He gave her an expansive grin that revealed good dentures. "You'd make a hell of a coach."

"Thanks." Pleased with the compliment, Brooke made her way toward the plate, and Parks. "You did very well."

He regarded her extended hand with amusement, but accepted it. "For a rookie?" he countered.

When she started to remove her hand, Parks held it firmly, running a light fingertip over the inside of her wrist. He had the satisfaction of feeling her pulse jump then speed up. "I didn't anticipate any problems, as you were simply playing yourself.'' Behind her, technicians were taking down lights and coiling cable. She heard E. J. describing the new lady he was seeing in glowing, if exaggerated, terms. Using all her willpower, Brooke concentrated on the background noises instead of the feel of Parks's finger tracing over her skin. ''The next scene should be fairly easy. We'll go over it on location this afternoon. If you have any questions—''

''Just one,'' Parks interrupted. ''Come here a minute.'' Without waiting for agreement, he drew her toward the dugout, stepped inside then just through the door that led to the locker rooms.

''What's the problem, Parks?'' Brooke demanded. ''I have to get into editing before the next shoot.''

''Are we finished here for now?''

With an impatient sigh, Brooke gestured to the equipment being packed. ''Obviously.''

''Fine.'' Pressing her back against the doorway, Parks covered her mouth with his.

It was a proprietary kiss with whispers of violence. The frustrations of the past hours seeped into it as he finally let them free. There was the annoyance of wanting her—of being too far away to touch for days, then being close enough, but not being permitted to. There was the exasperation of her cool professional treatment of him while he had fought an insistent growing desire. And there was the banked fury at being put in the position of taking orders from a woman who dominated his thoughts and denied his body.

Yet it was more agitating than soothing to press his body against the softness of hers. She filled him—the exotic scent, the ripe woman-taste of her mouth, the silken skin over the sharp, strong bones of her face.

Almost desperately, he pressed closer, plunged deeper. He would *not* be filled. He would find that corner, that secret place that would open her for him so that he could have her at last—body and mind. To do that he needed the edge of control, over himself, and over Brooke. Her strength made it a challenge—his desire made it a necessity.

"Hey, Brooke, want a ride to the . . . Whoops." E. J. poked his head into the dugout then quickly retreated. As Parks's lips freed hers, she could hear the cameraman whistling gleefully as he strolled away. Furious that she had completely lost track of time and place, Brooke shoved against Parks's chest.

"Let go of me!"

"Why?"

Apparently her ice-pick stare more amused than wounded him. "Don't you *ever* pull something like that when I'm working," she hissed, shoving a second time as Parks blocked her exit.

"I asked if we were finished," Parks reminded her, then backed her into the wall again.

"When we're on the job," Brooke said evenly, "I'm the director, you're the product." He narrowed his eyes at her choice of words, but she continued, full steam. "You'll do *exactly* what I tell you."

"The camera's not rolling, Brooke."

"I won't have my crew speculating, circulating gossip that can undermine my authority or my credibility."

His own temper rose in direct balance with need. She only aroused him more when she challenged. "Aren't you more afraid that you enjoy being touched by me? Doesn't it infuriate you that when I kiss you, you don't really give a damn who's in charge?" He bent his head so that his lips were only a breath from hers. "I took your orders all morning, Ms. Gordon. Now it's my turn."

Her lancelike stare didn't falter as the quiet words fluttered over her lips. With the tip of his tongue he traced them, enjoying their taste and her own suppressed passion. Merging desire stung the air—they both felt it, they both tried to rise above it in the struggle for dominance. Yet they both became aware that it was the desire that would win over each of them.

His lips rubbed over hers, without pressure or force, taunting her to demand he stop, daring her to resist her own needs. Their eyes remained open and fixed on each other. Both pair of irises darkened as passion tempted each of them to surrender.

"We have another shoot this afternoon," Brooke managed as she fought to keep her voice steady.

"When we're filming, I'll do what you tell me." He kissed her once, hard and quick. "Tonight," he added, dealing with his own heated blood, "we'll see."

Chapter 6

BROOKE CHOSE TO SHOOT DURING THE LATE-AFTERNOON
lull using day-for-night filters, rather than compete with
the evening traffic. It was a quick scene, relatively
simple and very glossy. The champagne-colored Rolls
would drive up in front of the posh restaurant, Parks
would alight, in the same outfit, but wearing a jacket—
already sponged and pressed from the morning—then
offer his hand to the sleekly dressed brunette. She would
step from the car, showing considerable leg, then flash
Parks a look before linking her arm through his. The
scene would then fade out, with Parks's voice-over
dubbed in, stating the motto for the campaign.

"De Marco. For the man who's going places."

The visual would be another twelve seconds, so that
combined with the stadium segment, the intro and the tag
at the end, the commercial would round out at thirty
seconds.

"I want a long shot of the Rolls, E. J., then come in on Parks as he steps out. We don't want to lose the impact that he's wearing the same outfit he played ball in. Don't get hung up on the lady," she added dryly as she sent him a knowing look.

"Who me?" Pulling a Kings fielder's cap out of his back pocket, he offered it to Brooke. "Want to wear it? Team spirit?"

Placing one hand on her hip, Brooke stared at him without any change of expression. With a quick chuckle, E. J. fit the cap over his own modified Afro.

"Okay, boss, I'm ready when you are."

As was her habit, Brooke rechecked the camera angle and the lighting before she signaled the first take. The Rolls cruised sedately to the curb. Brooke played the background music over in her head, trying to judge how it would fit. On cue, Parks climbed out, turning to offer his hand to the brunette still inside. Frowning, Brooke let the scene play out. It wasn't right. She saw why immediately but took the few minutes until the cut to work out how to approach Parks.

With a gesture, Brooke indicated that she would speak to Parks while the driver backed up the Rolls for the next take. Putting a hand on his arm, she led him away from the technicians. "Parks, you have to relax." Because handling fidgety actors was second nature to her, Brooke's voice and manner were markedly different from the morning session. Parks noted it and bristled anyway.

"I don't know what you mean."

She steered him well away from where a few interested pedestrians were loitering by a barricade. "Number one," she began, "you're plugging a good product. Try to believe in it."

"If I didn't think it was a good product, I wouldn't be doing this," he retorted, frowning over her shoulder at the huddle of lights.

"But you're not comfortable." When Brooke gave his shoulder a reassuring pat, Parks scowled at her. "If you insist on feeling like an idiot, it's going to show. Wait," she ordered as he started to speak. "This morning, you felt more at ease—the stadium, a bat in your hand. After the first couple of minutes, you started to play the game. That's all I want you to do now."

"Look, Brooke, I'm not an actor—"

"Who's asking you to act?" she countered. "God spare me from that." She knew she'd insulted him, so she tempered the comment with a smile. "Listen, you're a winner, out on the town in a chauffeured Rolls with a gorgeous woman. All I want you to do is have a good time and look rather pleased with yourself. You can pull it off, Parks. Loosen up."

"I wonder how you'd feel if someone asked you to field a line drive with twenty thousand people watching."

Brooke smiled again and tried not to think about the minutes ticking away. "You do that routinely," she pointed out, "because you concentrate on your job and forget those thousands of people."

"This is different," he muttered.

"Only if you let it be. Just let me see that same self-satisfied look on your face that you had when you hit that homer this morning. Pretend, Parks." Brooke straightened the collar of his shirt. "It's good for you."

"Did you know that Nina has the IQ of a soft-boiled egg?"

"Nina?"

"My date."

Brooke gave in to a sigh. "Stop being so temperamental; nobody's asking you to marry her."

Parks opened his mouth, then shut it again. No one had ever accused him of being temperamental. He'd never *been* temperamental. If his manager told him to take a three-and-one pitch, he took it. If the third base coach told him to steal home, he ran. Not because he was malleable, but because if he was signed with a team, he followed the rules. It didn't mean he always had to like them. With a quiet oath, he ran a hand through his hair and admitted that it wasn't so much what the orders were in this case, but who was laying them out. But then, the lights and cameras would eventually shut down.

"Fine, let's do it again." He gave Brooke the slow smile she'd learned not to trust before he walked toward the Rolls. Suspicious of his easy capitulation, Brooke turned back to stand behind E. J.

Parks gave her no more cause to complain, though they were more than two hours shooting the segment. Brooke found that she had more trouble with the professional actress—and a couple of fans who recognized Parks—than she had with him. It took three takes before she convinced Nina that she wasn't looking for glowing and adoring, but for sleek and aloof. Brooke wanted the contrast and ran everyone through the twelve seconds until she was certain she had it.

Then there was the matter of the two fans who sneaked through the barricade to get Parks's autograph while the camera was still rolling. Parks obliged them, and though Brooke simmered at the interruption, she noted that he dispatched the fans with the charm of a seasoned diplomat. Grudgingly, she had to admit she couldn't have done better herself.

"That's a wrap," Brooke announced, arching her back. She'd been on her feet for over eight hours, bolting down a half a sandwich between segments. She felt pleased with the day's work, satisfied with Parks's progress and ravenous. "You can break down," she told the crew. "Good job. E. J., I've scheduled the editing and dubbing for tomorrow. If you want to see what we're going to do to your film, you can come in."

"It's Saturday."

"Yeah." She pulled the bill of the fielder's cap over his face. "We'll start working at ten. Nina . . ." Brooke took the actress's slim, smooth hand. "You were lovely, thank you. Fred, make sure the Rolls gets back in one piece, or you'll have to face Claire. Bigelow, what's the new kid's name?" Brooke jerked her head at a young technician who was busily packing up lights.

"Silbey?"

With a nod, Brooke made a mental note of it. "He's good," she said briefly, then turned to Parks. "Well, you made it through the first one. We'll dub in the voice-over tomorrow. Any scars?"

"None that show."

"Maybe I shouldn't tell you that this one is the easiest on the schedule."

He met the humor in her eyes blandly. "Maybe you shouldn't."

"Where's your car?"

"Out at the stadium."

With a frown, Brooke checked her watch. "I'll give you a lift back there." She toyed with the idea of going by Thorton's first to take a quick look at the film, then discarded the idea. It would be better to look at it fresh in the morning. "I have to call Claire. . . . Well." Brooke shrugged. "That can wait. Any problems?" she asked to the crew in general.

"Tomorrow's Saturday," an aggrieved E. J. stated again as he packed up his equipment. "Woman, you just don't give a man a break."

"You don't have to come in," she reminded him, knowing he would. "Good night." With Parks beside her, Brooke started down the street.

"Do you make a habit of working weekends?" he asked, noting that after a long, hectic day she still moved as though she had urgent appointments to keep.

"When it's necessary. We're rushing this through to get it aired during the play-offs or, barring that, the series." She shot him a look. "You'd better be in it." Still walking, she began to dig in the purse slung over her shoulder.

"I'll try to accommodate you. Want me to drive?"

With the keys in one hand, Brooke looked up in surprise. "Have you been talking to E. J.?"

His brows drew together. "No. Why?"

"Nothing." Dismissing the thought, Brooke paused beside her car. "Why do you want to drive?"

"It occurs to me that I may have had to stand in front of that stupid camera off and on all day, but you haven't stopped for over eight hours. It's a tough job."

"I'm a tough lady," she responded with a trace of defensiveness in her voice.

"Yeah." He grazed his knuckles over her cheek. "Iron."

"Just get in the car," Brooke muttered. After rounding the hood, she climbed in, slamming the door only slightly. "It'll take a little while to get across town in this traffic."

"I'm not in a hurry." Parks settled comfortably beside her. "Can you cook?"

In the act of starting the car, Brooke frowned at him. "Can I what?"

"Cook. You know." Parks pantomimed the act of stirring a pan.

She laughed, shooting out into traffic with an exuberance that made Parks wince. "Of course I can cook."

"How about your place?"

Brooke zipped through a yellow light. "What about my place?" she asked cautiously.

"For dinner." Parks watched her shift into third as she scooted around a Porsche. "It seems to me I'm entitled after feeding you a couple times myself."

"You want me to cook for you?"

This time he laughed. She was going to fight him right down to the wire. "Yeah. And then I'm going to make love to you."

Brooke hit the brakes, stopping the car inches away from another bumper. "Oh, really?"

"Oh, really," he repeated, meeting her dagger-eyed stare equably. "We both just punched out on the time clock. New game." He fingered the end of her braid. "New rules."

"And if I have some objection?"

"Why don't we talk about it someplace quiet?" With his thumb, he traced her lips. "Not afraid, are you?"

The taunt was enough. When the light changed, Brooke hit the accelerator, weaving through Los Angeles traffic with grim determination.

"Did you know that you drive like a maniac?" Parks observed.

"Yes."

"Just a passing comment," he murmured, then settled back against the seat.

Despite the infuriated woman beside him, Parks had the same sensation of tranquillity when Brooke zoomed up in her driveway, braking with a teeth-jarring jolt, that he had had the first time he had seen her house. There was a tang of fall in the air—that spicy, woodsy fragrance you never smelled in Los Angeles. Some of the leaves had turned so that splashes of red and amber and orange competed with the customary California green. The shadows of trees reflected in the glass of the windows as the sun dipped lower in the sky. Along the base of the house the flowers had been allowed to grow bushy and wild. Whether it had been by intent or lack of time, her unkempt garden was eye-catching and perfectly suited to the lonely mountain spot.

Without a word, Brooke slammed out of her side of the car. At a more leisurely pace, Parks followed suit. She was furious, Parks noted with a pleased grin. All the better. He didn't want an easy capitulation. From the first moment he had come into contact with her, he had looked forward to the struggle almost as much as he had looked forward to the outcome. He'd never had any doubt what that would be. When there was this much friction, and this much spark between a man and a woman, they became enemies or lovers. He had no intention of being Brooke's enemy.

Still keeping her stony silence, Brooke slipped the key into the lock and turned it. Walking inside, she left him to follow as he chose.

The fireplace caught his eye first. It was crafted from large stone, dominating one wall. The fire set was shiny brass, though dented and obviously old. Another wall was all glass, rising from either side of the door to the peak of the roof. Gazing at it, he felt not a loss of privacy but a basic sense of security. Rocking gently on his heels, he studied the rest of the main room.

A long armless sofa ranged in front of the fireplace, crowded with dozens of pillows. In lieu of a table a large, round hassock sat in front of it. Around this focal point a few chairs were scattered. All the colors were muted—ecrus, buffs, biscuits—set off by the surprising touches of huge, brilliant peacock feathers in a brass urn, a scarlet afghan tossed over the back of a chair, the vivid shades in the hooked rug on the planked floor.

A shelf had been built into the east wall. Ignoring Brooke's glare, Parks wandered to it. There was a small crystal butterfly that shivered in a rainbow of colors as the light struck it. There was a chipped demitasse set that had come from one of Brooke's yard sale jaunts along with a fat, grinning bear. Parks noted a piece of Wedgewood next to a pink monkey holding cymbals. It clapped them together gleefully when he flipped a switch. With a quick laugh, he flipped it off again. There were other treasures scattered haphazardly through the room, some priceless, some no more than department store whimsy.

Above his head, the second-floor balcony ran the length of the house. No closed-in spaces, he noted. He began to think the house itself would tell him more about Brooke than she would volunteer. The need for freedom of movement, the eclectic tastes, the combination of drab colors with the garish. It occurred to him that everything she owned would have been collected during the last ten years. But how much of the past had she brought with her?

Uncomfortable with Parks's silent, thorough survey, Brooke marched to a tiny corner cabinet to pull out a bottle. "You're free to take a tour," she said abruptly. "I'm going to have a drink."

"Whatever you're having's fine," Parks said with infuriating amiability. "You can show me around later." He proceeded to make himself at home on the low, spreading sofa. Leaning back, he glanced at the fireplace, observing by the ash that Brooke made good use of it. "Fire'd be nice," he said casually. "Got any wood?"

"Out back." Ungraciously, she stuck a glass under his nose.

"Thanks." After accepting it, Parks took her hand. "Sit down," he invited with a pleasantness that put Brooke's teeth on edge. "You've been on your feet all day."

"I'm fine," she began, then let out a gasp of surprise as Parks yanked her down beside him. Realizing she should have been prepared for the move despite his outward mellowness only fanned her already strained temper. "Who do you think you are," she began, "barging in here, expecting me to whip up dinner then fall into bed with you? If you—"

"Hungry?" Parks interrupted.

She sent him a searing look. "No."

With a shrug, he draped his arm behind her, propping his feet on the hassock. "You're usually ill-tempered when you are," he commented.

"I am *not* ill-tempered," Brooke raged. "And I am *not* hungry."

"Want some music?"

Brooke drew in a deep breath. How dare he sit there acting as though she were *his* guest? "No."

"You should relax." With firm fingers, he began to knead the base of her neck.

"I'm perfectly relaxed." She pushed his hand aside, disturbed by the sensation of warmth creeping down her spine.

"Brooke." Parks set his glass on the floor, then turned to her. "When you called me a few days ago, you accepted what you knew was going to happen between us."

"I said I would see you," she corrected and started to rise. Parks hand came back to her neck and held her still.

"Knowing what *seeing* me meant," he murmured. His eyes met the fury in her gaze for a moment, then drifted down to focus on her mouth. "You might have refused to let me come here tonight . . . but you didn't." Slowly, he brought his eyes back to hers in a long, intense look that had her stomach muscles quivering. "Are you going to tell me that you don't want me?"

She couldn't remember the last time she had felt the need to break eye contact. It took all her strength of will to keep from faltering. "I . . . I don't have to tell you anything. You might remember that this is my time, my house. And—"

"What are you afraid of?"

As he watched, the confusion in her eyes turned back to fury. "I'm not afraid of anything."

"Of making love to me," he continued quietly. "Or to anyone?"

Angry color flooded her cheeks as she bolted up from the sofa. She felt a combination of rage and hurt and fear that she hadn't experienced in more than a decade. He had no right to bring the insecurity tumbling back over her, no right to make her doubt herself as a woman. Tossing her head, Brooke glared at him. "You want to make love?" she snapped. "Fine." She turned on her heel and marched to the stairs leading to the second floor. Halfway up, she threw an angry look over her shoulder. "Coming?" she demanded, then continued on without waiting for his reply.

The fury carried her across the balcony and into her bedroom, where she stood in the center of the room, seething. Her gaze landed on the bed, but she averted it quickly as she heard the sound of Parks's footsteps approaching. It was all very simple, she told herself. They would go to bed and work this attraction or animosity or whatever it was out of their systems. It would clear the air. She sent Parks another killing look as he walked into the room. Fear prodded at her again. In defense, Brooke hastily began to undress.

It was on the tip of his tongue to tell her to stop, then Parks calmly followed her example. She was trembling and didn't even know it, he observed. For the moment, they would play it her way. As with the first night he had taken her out, Parks knew what Brooke expected. Though the angry fear urged him to comfort, he was aware that it would be refused. He didn't even glance over when she dropped her T-shirt into a heap on the floor. But he noticed that she had kept a small clutch of his hibiscus on her dresser.

Naked, Brooke stomped over to the bed and pulled off the quilt. Head high, brows arched, she turned to him. "Well?"

He looked at her. The surge of sharp desire caused him to go rigid to control it. She was long and softly rounded with fragile, china-doll skin. The proud almost challenging stance was only accented by the overall frailty—until one looked at her eyes. Stormy, they dared him to make the next move.

Parks wondered if she knew just how vulnerable she was and vowed, even as he planned to conquer, to protect. Taking his time, he walked to her until they stood face-to-face. Though her eyes never faltered, he saw the quick nervous swallow before she turned toward the bed. Parks caught her braid in his hand, forcing her to turn back. The fury in her eyes might have cooled the desire of most men. Parks smiled, comfortable with it.

"This time," he murmured as he began to unbind the braid, "I'll direct."

Brooke stood stiffly as he slowly freed her hair. Her skin tingled, as if waiting for his touch—but he never touched her. Deliberately, Parks drew out the process, working his way leisurely up the confined hair until Brooke thought she would burst. When he had finished, he spread it over her shoulders as if it were the only task he would ever perform.

"It's fabulous," Parks murmured, absorbed in its texture, at the way the slanting sunlight brought out the hidden gold within the red. Lifting a strand from her shoulder, he buried his nose in it, wanting to absorb the fragrance. Brooke felt her knees weaken, her muscles go lax. Would he ever touch her?

She kept her eyes on his face, trying to avoid a dangerous fascination with the tawny skin of his chest, the mat of dark-gold hair and cords of muscles she had glimpsed in his bare shoulders. If she allowed herself to look, would she be able to prevent herself from touching? But when she noticed the thin gold chain around his neck, curiosity drove her to follow it down to the small gold circle that dangled from it. Because of this, she didn't see him shift ever so slightly to press his lips against the curve of her shoulder. The touch was a jolt, a branding shock that had her jerking back even as his hands spanned her waist.

"Relax." Fingers kneaded gently into flesh; warm lips nibbled it over his words. "I won't take you anywhere you don't want to go." Slowly, he ran the whisper-soft kisses over her shoulder, loitering at her throat. His fingertips ran down to her hips then back up in a rhythmic caress that could never soothe, but only arouse. He knew what he did to her—she knew her response was no secret. In a last attempt to hold her own, Brooke pressed her hands against his chest, arching back.

Parks still held her waist, but made no attempt to draw her back. Over the desire in his eyes, Brooke caught the light of humor. "Want me to stop?" he asked quietly. There was a trace of challenge in the question. She realized abruptly that whatever response she gave, she would still lose.

"Would you?" she countered, fighting the urge to run her suddenly sensitive fingertips over his naked chest.

It was his slow, dangerous smile. "Why don't you ask

me and see?'' Even as she opened her mouth to form an answer, his fastened on it. The kiss was soft and deep, the sort she knew a woman could drown in. Brooke had only the vague realization that her hands had crept up his chest to link around his neck, only the faintest knowledge that her body was melting into his. Then she was falling—or perhaps she was drowning—until the cool sheets were under her back and his weight was on her.

She didn't question how her body seemed to have become liquid, only reveled in the unaccustomed freedom of motion and space. His hands were so sure, so unhurried, as if he wished and waited for her total fluidity. With a deft caress, a strategic brush of lips, he was unlocking every restriction she had placed on herself. This pleasure was thick, fluent. Brooke luxuriated in it, no longer caring what she gave up in order to receive. Weightless, helpless, she could only sigh as he took his mouth on a lazy journey down her body.

The flick of his tongue over her nipple brought a quick tug—not quite an ache—in her stomach. This pleasure was sharp, stunning. Then it was gone, leaving her dazed as he continued to range a moist trail over her.

His hands were never still, but moved so gently, almost magically, over her, that she could never pinpoint where the source of delight came from. It seemed to radiate through the whole of her, soothing, promising, luring. He caught the point of her breast between his teeth, causing a flash of heat to spring from her center out to her fingertips. But even as she gasped from it, arching, he moved on. He brushed his fingers over her inner thigh, almost absently, so that her skin was left heated then chilled. As fire and ice coursed through her, the sound of her own moan echoed in her head.

The quivering started—a drug wearing off. And the ache—unbearable, wonderful. She was no longer soothed, but throbbing and pleasure became exquisite torment. Suddenly her fingers were in his hair as she tried to press him closer. "Make love to me," she demanded as her breath started to tremble.

He continued with the same mind-destroying caresses. "Oh, I am," he murmured.

"Now." Brooke reached for him only to have him grip her wrists. His head lifted so that their eyes met. Even through a haze of passion she could see his intense concentration—that fierce warrior look.

"It's not so simple." He could feel her pulse hammering under his fingers, but he would give her no quick moment of pleasure. When he took her, she would never forget. Parks pressed his mouth to hers, not so gently. "I've only begun."

Still holding her wrists, he began a new journey over her, with his mouth only. As he captured her breast again, taking it into the heated moistness of his mouth, she could only writhe beneath him in a frenzy that had nothing to do with a desire to escape. The breezy patience had left him to be replaced by a demand that would accept only one answer. It seemed he would feed on her skin, nipping, suckling, licking until she was half-mad from need so long suppressed. It seemed he would taste, and taste only, for hours, assuaging a steady greed she was powerless to refuse.

The heat suffused her, enervated her. Her skin trembled and grew moist from it. Down the hollow between her breasts, over the lean line of ribs to the subtle curve of hip he traced kisses until he felt her hands go limp and her pulse rage.

When his tongue plunged into the warm core of her, she shuddered convulsively, crying out with the first delirious peak. But he was relentless. Even as she struggled for breath, his hands began a new journey of possession.

With hers free, Brooke gripped his shoulders, hardly aware of the tensing of his muscles. There was no part of her body he hadn't explored, exploited, in his quest to have all of her. Now her surrender became agility and drive. Neither of them knew that her true capitulation came when she began her own demands.

Her hands sped over him, touching all she could reach while she twisted, wanting to taste—his mouth, his shoulder, the strong line of jaw. Parks thought her scent intensified until it dominated all his senses—weakening and strengthening him at once. Her skin was moist and heated wherever his mouth nestled, bringing him another tantalizing image of white silk and forbidden passion. Husky murmurs and quick breathing broke the early-evening hush.

He was no longer thinking, nor was she. They had entered a place where thoughts were only sensations; sharp, aching, sweet and dark. Even as she fastened her mouth on his, Brooke trembled.

Then he was deep inside her, so swiftly that she dug her nails into his flesh in shock and pleasure. They merged, body to body, heart to heart, while all the sensations concentrated into one.

Chapter 7

BROOKE LUXURIATED IN THE SOFT, WARM SECURITY. As she hung between sleep and wakefulness she thought it was winter, and that she slept beneath a thick downy quilt. There was no need to get up, no need to face the cold. She could lay there for a whole lazy day and do nothing. She felt utterly peaceful, completely unburdened and pleasantly languid. Wanting to enjoy the sensations more, she struggled to shrug off sleep.

It wasn't winter, but early fall. There was no quilt, only a tangle of sheet that half covered her naked body as she curled into Parks. With sleep cleared from her mind, Brooke remembered everything—the first revelation of lovemaking, the surprise of having the secret door open without resistance, the hours of passion that had followed. There had been little talk, as the urgency to give and take had grown beyond the control of either of them. Time after time, fulfillment had led to rekindled desire, and desire to demand, until they had fallen asleep, wrapped tightly together.

Now, Brooke could remember her own insatiable thirst, the boundless energy and strength that had filled her. She remembered, too, Parks's ability to arouse her to desperation with patience . . . and that she had driven him beyond patience with a skill she had been unaware of possessing. But beyond the passion and pleasure, Brooke remembered one vital thing. She had needed him. This was something she had refused herself for years. To need meant dependence, dependence meant vulnerability. A woman who was vulnerable would always be hurt.

The night was behind her and dawn was breaking. In the misty gray light, Parks's face was relaxed, inches from hers, so that the warmth of his breath fluttered over her cheek. His arm was around her, his fingers curled into her hair, as if even in sleep he had to touch it. Her arm reached around to lock him close. They had slept, if only for a few hours, in a classic pose of possessing and possessed. But which one, Brooke thought hazily, was which?

With a sigh, Brooke closed her eyes. Not knowing was dangerous. The hours she had spent not caring put the independence she had taken for granted in jeopardy.

It was time to think again before it was too late, before emotions dominated her—those perilous emotions that urged her to burrow closer to Parks's warmth. If she were ever to stop the need for him from growing beyond her control, she had to do it now.

Brooke shifted in an attempt to separate her body from his. Parks tightened his hold and only brought her closer. "No," he murmured without opening his eyes. With sleepy slowness he ran his hand down the length of her naked back. "Too early to get up."

Brooke felt her breasts yield against his chest, felt the warmth in her stomach begin to smolder to heat. His lips were close—too close. The need to stay in the security of his arms was so strong it frightened her. Again Brooke tried to shift, and again Parks brought her back.

"Parks," she began, then was silenced by his lips.

Brooke told herself to struggle against the deep, musky morning kiss, but she didn't. She told herself to resist the gentle play of fingertips on her spine, but she couldn't. The gray dawn suddenly took on a rose hue. The air seemed to grow thick. Even as he touched her, her skin quivered to be touched again. Don't! her brain shouted. Don't let this happen. But she was already sinking, and sinking quickly. She made a sound of protest that became a groan of pleasure.

Parks shifted so that his body lay across hers. Burying his face in her hair, he took his hand down the length of her; the slight swell of the side of her breast, the firm line of ribs and narrow waist, a flare of hip and long smooth thigh. He could feel the struggle going on inside her, sense her desire to separate herself from what had begun to happen between them since that first meeting of eyes. His quick flash of anger was tinged with unexpected hurt.

"Regrets already?" Lifting his head, he looked at her. Her eyes were dark, heavy with kindling passion. Her breathing was unsteady. But he knew she fought herself just as fiercely as she fought him. Her hands were on his shoulders, poised to push him away.

"This isn't smart," Brooke managed.

"No?" Controlling anger, ignoring the hurt, Parks brushed the hair from her cheek. "Why?"

Brooke met his eyes, because to look away would have admitted defeat. "It's not what I want."

"Let's be accurate." His voice was calm, his eyes steady. "It's not what you want to want."

"All right." Brooke shivered as his finger traced her ear. "It's not what I want to want. I have to be practical. We're going to be working together for quite a while. More technically, you'll be working for me. A solid professional relationship won't be possible if we're lovers."

"We are lovers," Parks pointed out, casually shifting so that the friction of his body on hers sent a shudder coursing through her.

"It won't be possible," Brooke continued, concentrating on keeping her voice steady, "if we go on being lovers."

Tilting his head, Parks smiled at her. "Why?"

"Because . . ." Brooke knew why. She knew dozens of logical reasons why, but no firm thought would form in her brain when he touched a light friendly kiss to her lips.

"Let me be practical a minute," Parks said after another quick kiss. "How often do you let yourself have fun?"

Brooke drew her brows together in annoyed confusion. "What do you mean?"

"You can work eight, twelve hours a day," Parks continued. "You can enjoy your job, be terrific at what you do, but you still need to throw a Frisbee now and again."

"Frisbee?" This brought on a baffled laugh that pleased him. The hands on his shoulders relaxed. "What are you talking about?"

"Fun, Brooke. A sense of the ridiculous, laziness, riding Ferris wheels. All those things that make working worthwhile."

She had the uncomfortable feeling she was being expertly led away from the subject at hand. "What does riding a Ferris wheel have to do with you and me making love?"

"Have you ever had a lover before?" Parks felt her stiffen but continued. "I don't mean someone you slept with, but someone you shared time with. I'm not asking you for any more than that." Even as he said it, Parks knew it wouldn't be true for long. He would ask for more, and she would fight him every step of the way. But then he had lived his life playing to win. "Throw a few Frisbees with me, Brooke. Ride a few waves. Let's see where it takes us."

Looking at him, she could feel her resistance melting. Before she could prevent it, her hand had lifted from his shoulder to brush at the hair that fell over his forehead. "You make it sound so simple," she murmured.

"Not simple." He took her other hand and pressed his lips to the palm. "Even fun isn't always simple. I want you . . . here." And his eyes came back to hers. "Naked, warm, daring me to arouse you. I want to drive with you with the top down and the wind in your hair. I want to see you caught in the rain, laughing." He ran whispering kisses over her face, then paused at her lips to drink long and deep. "I want to be with you, but I don't think it's going to be simple."

Rolling over, Parks cradled her head on his chest,

allowing her to rest and think while he brushed his hands through her hair. His words had touched her in tiny vulnerable places she couldn't defend. Was she strong enough, she wondered, to try things his way without losing control? Fun, she thought. Yes, they could give each other that. He challenged her. Brooke had to admit that she had come to enjoy even the friction. What had he said once? That they could be friends before they were lovers. Odd, she mused, that both had happened almost before she realized it. Only the niggling fear that she was already afraid of losing him kept her from relaxing completely.

"I can't afford to fall in love with you," she murmured.

An odd way to put it, Parks reflected as he continued to stroke her hair. "Rule one," he drawled, "Party A will not fall in love with Party B."

Making a fist, Brooke punched his shoulder. "Stop making me sound ridiculous."

"I'll try," he agreed amiably.

"Fun," she murmured, half to herself.

"A three-letter word meaning amusement, sport or recreation," Parks recited in a blandly didactic tone.

With a chuckle, Brooke lifted her head. "All right. I'll buy the Frisbee," she said before she pressed her mouth to his.

Parks cupped the back of her neck in his hand. "It's still too early to get up," he murmured.

Brooke's low laugh was muffled against his lips. "I'm not sleepy."

With a reluctant sigh, he closed his eyes. "Acting," he said thickly, "takes a lot out of you."

"Aw." Sympathetically, Brooke stroked his cheek.

"I guess you'd better conserve your strength." She pressed a kiss to his jaw, then his collarbone, before continuing down his chest. Her fingers tangled with the gold chain he wore. "What's this for?"

Parks opened one eye to stare at the five-dollar gold piece that dangled from the chain Brooke held up. "Luck." He shut his eyes again. "My aunt gave it to me when I headed for the Florida training camp. She told my father he was a"—Parks reached back in his memory for the exact phrasing—"a stiff-necked old fool who thought in graphs and formulas, then gave me the gold piece and told me to go for it."

Brooke turned the shiny circle over in her palm. So he carried a little piece of the past with him, too, she mused. "Superstition?" she asked as she dropped the chain and pressed her lips to his chest.

"Luck," Parks corrected, enjoying the feel of her mouth on his skin, "has nothing to do with superstition."

"I see." She scraped her nails lightly down his side and heard his quick inhalation of breath. "Do you always wear it?"

"Mmm." She flicked her tongue over his nipple, bringing a low, involuntary groan from him. A sense of power whipped through her—light, freeing, tempting. His hands were buried in her hair again, seeking the flesh beneath. Brooke slid her body down, bringing them both a rippling slice of pleasure.

His scent was different, she discovered as she ran her lips over his skin. Different, she realized, because hers had mingled with it during the night. That was intimacy, as tangible as the act of love itself.

As the power stayed with her, she experimented. His

body was strong and muscled beneath hers, tasting of man. He was taut and lean, his skin golden in the early-morning light. The palms that moved over her back were hard, calloused from his profession. Like the man, the body was disciplined, a product of that odd combination of pampering and outrageous demands any athlete subjects it to. She brushed her lips over the hard, flat stomach and felt the firm muscles quiver. Beneath her own smooth palms she could feel the sinewy strength of his thighs.

The knowledge of the pure physical strength he possessed excited her. With light touches and caresses, she could make this man breathe as though he had run to the point of collapse. With feathering kisses she could make this hardened athlete shudder with an inner weakness she alone was aware of. Though she didn't fully understand it, Brooke knew that she had given him something more than her body the night before, something more complex than surrender or passion. Without even knowing what the gift was, she wanted Parks to offer it in return.

Slowly, enjoying every movement of his body beneath hers, savoring each subtly different taste, she roamed up until her lips fastened greedily on his. How soft his mouth was. How nectarous, with a dark, secret cachet. Brooke savored it on her tongue, feeling it intensify until the draining, liquefying pleasure crept into her. Knowing she would lose that slim edge of control, she tore her mouth from his to bury it at his throat.

She felt the vibration of his groan against her lips, but she couldn't hear it. Her heartbeat raged in her head until all of her senses were confused. If it was morning, how could she feel this sultry night pleasure? If she was seducing him, how was she so thoroughly seduced? Her body pressed against his, matching itself to the slow, tortuous rhythm he set even as she raced tormenting kisses along his flesh. The heat seeping into her only seemed to add to the delirium of power, yet it wasn't enough. She was still searching for something so nebulous she wasn't certain she would recognize it when it was found. And desire, sharp bolts of desire, were causing everything but the quest for fulfillment to fade.

Parks gripped her hair in one hand to pull her head up. She had only a brief glimpse of his face—the eyes half-shut but darker and more intense than she had ever seen them—before he brought her mouth down to his and devoured. All will, all sense was seeping out of her.

"Brooke . . ." His hands were on her hips, urging her. "Now." The demand was wrenched from him, hoarse and urgent. She resisted, struggling to breathe, fighting to hold some part of herself separate. "I need you," he murmured before their lips met again. "I need you."

Then it was clear—for one breathless instant. She needed, and knew now she was needed in return. It was enough . . . perhaps everything. With a shuddering sound of relief and joy, she gave.

At nine fifty-five, Claire swept into the editing room. Neither the editors nor E. J. were surprised to see the head of Thorton Productions on the job on a Saturday morning. Anyone who had worked at Thorton more than a week knew that Claire wasn't a figurehead but an entity to be reckoned with. She wore one of her trim little suits, the color of crushed raspberries, and a trace of Parisian scent.

"Dave, Lila, E. J." Claire gave all three a quick nod before heading toward the coffeepot. A newer member of the staff might have scurried to serve the boss, but those lounging near the control board knew better.

"Made it myself, Ms. Thorton," E. J. told her as she poured. "It won't taste like the battery acid these two cook up."

"I appreciate that, E. J.," she said dryly. Just the scent of it revived her. Claire inhaled it, telling herself only an old fool thought she could dance until three and still function the next day. Ah, but how nice it was to feel like a fool again, she thought with a slow smile. "I'm told that the shoot went well, with no major problems."

"Smooth as silk," E. J. stated. "Wait till you get a load of Parks knocking that sucker over the fence." He grinned reminiscently. "I won ten bucks off Brooke with that hit." His selective memory allowed him to forget that it had been his ten dollars in the first place.

Claire settled into a chair with a quiet sigh. "Is Brooke in yet?"

"Haven't seen her." E. J. began to whistle as he recalled Brooke leaving the location with Parks. Accustomed to his habits, Claire only lifted a brow.

"Are you set up, Dave?"

"Ready to run through it, Ms. Thorton. Want to see it from the top?"

"In a moment." Even as Claire checked her watch, she heard Brooke's voice in the corridor.

"As long as you understand you have absolutely no say in what gets cut and what stays in."

"I might have an intelligent comment to make."

"Parks, I'm serious."

His low chuckle rolled into the editing room just ahead of Brooke. "Morning," she said to the group at large. "Coffee hot?"

"E. J.'s special," Claire told her, watching Brooke over the rim of her mug as she sipped. She looked different, Claire thought, then slid her eyes to Parks. And there was the reason, she concluded with a small smile. "Good morning, Parks."

Her face remained bland and friendly, but he recognized her thoughts. With a slight nod, he acknowledged them. "Hello, Claire," he said, abandoning formality as smoothly as he reached for a cup for himself. "I hope you don't mind me sitting in on this." Taking the pot, he poured Brooke's coffee, then his own. "Brooke has a few reservations."

"Amateurs," Brooke said precisely as she reached for the powdered cream, "have a tendency to be pains in the—"

"Yes, well I'm sure we're delighted to have Parks join us," Claire interrupted over E. J.'s chuckle. "Run it through, Dave. Let's see what we've got."

At her order, he flicked a series of buttons on the large control panel in front of him. Parks watched himself appear simultaneously on three monitors. He could hear Brooke's voice off camera, then the little man with the clapboard scooted in front of him announcing the scene and take.

"It's the third take that worked," Brooke announced as she settled on the arm of Claire's chair. "Casey at the bat didn't like the first pitch."

Her remark earned her a grin from Parks and a mild exclamation from Claire. "The lighting's very good." Claire studied the second take through narrowed eyes.

"The new boy, Silbey. He's got a nice touch. The clothes sell it." Brooke sipped while gesturing with her free hand. "Watch when he sets for the swing. . . . Yes." She gave a nod of approval. "Nice moves, no apparent restriction. He looks comfortable, efficient, sexy." Intent on the screen, Brooke didn't notice the look Parks tossed at her. "This is the one I want to use." She waited, silently, watching the replay of Parks's home run. The test swings, the concentration, the connection and follow-through, the satisfied grin and the shrug.

"I want to keep in the last bit," Brooke went on. "That gee-whiz shrug. It sells the whole business. That natural cockiness is its own appeal." Parks choked over his coffee, but Brooke ignored him. "As I see it, this segment is pretty clear-cut. The next I'm not so sure about. It's going to be effective. . . ."

Cupping his mug in both hands, Parks sat down. For the next two hours he watched himself on the screens of the monitors, listened to himself being weighed, dissected, judged. Though the latter disconcerted him initially, he found that watching himself didn't bring on the feeling of idiocy he'd been certain it would. He began to think he might find some enjoyment out of his two-year stint after all.

Though he'd heard himself picked apart and put back together countless times over the years—coaches, sports critics, other players—Parks couldn't find the same level of tolerance at hearing Brooke speak so matter-of-factly

about his face and body, his gestures and expressions.
All in all, he thought, it was as though he were the
salable product, not the clothes he wore.

They ran the film back and forth, while Claire listened
to input and made occasional comments. Yes, they
would have to work in close-ups in the next shoot, his
face was very good. It would be smart to fill another
thirty-second spot with action to exploit the way he
moved, showing the durability of the clothes as well as
the versatility. They might try tennis shorts if his legs
were any good.

At this Parks shot Brooke a deadly glance, half
expecting her to offer her personal opinion. She caught
it, then smothered a chuckle with a fit of coughing. Over
Claire's head she gave him an innocent smile and an
unexpectedly lewd wink. The quick response of his own
body caused him to scowl at her. She was dressed like a
waif, in baggy chinos and a sweater, her hair braided
back and secured with a rubber band. From across the
room he could smell the elusive, promising scent of her
perfume.

"We taped his voice-over this morning," she told
Claire. "I think you'll find his voice is good, though
how he'll handle real dialogue remains to be seen. Do we
have the graphics for the tag-on, Lila?"

"Right here." She flipped a series of switches. On the
monitor now was the de Marco logo of a black-maned
lion against a cool-blue background. The signature line
cartwheeled slowly onto the screen until it stopped
below the cat. It held long enough for impact, then
faded.

"Very classy," Brooke approved. "Then it's agreed?

The third take from the first segment, the fifth from the second.''

"We saved you guys from a lot of splicing," E. J. commented as he toyed with an unlit cigarette. "You should be able to put this together with your eyes closed."

"I'd appreciate it if you'd keep them open," Claire said as she rose. "Let me know when it's cut and dubbed. E. J., a splendid job, as always.''

"Thanks, Ms. Thorton."

She handed him her empty mug. "On the camera-work, too," she added. The editors snickered as she turned toward the door. "Parks, I hope you didn't find all this too boring."

"On the contrary . . ." He thought of the objective discussions on his anatomy. "It's been an education."

She gave him a mild smile of perfect understanding. "Brooke, my office, ten minutes." As an afterthought she glanced at her watch. "Oh, dear. Perhaps you'd like to join us for lunch, Parks."

"I appreciate it, but I have a few things I have to do."

"Well then." Patting his arm, she smiled again. "Best of luck in the play-offs." She slipped away, leaving Brooke frowning after her.

"I probably won't get any lunch now," she muttered. "If you'd said yes, she'd have made reservations at Ma Maison."

"Sorry." Parks drew her out in the corridor. "Did that wink mean you approve of my legs?"

"Wink?" Brooke stared at him blankly. "I don't know what you're talking about. Winking during an editing session is very unprofessional."

He glanced at the door she had closed behind her. "The way you all talked in there, I felt that I was the product."

With a half laugh, Brooke shook her head. "Parks, you *are* the product."

His eyes came back to hers, surprising Brooke with the flare of anger. "No. I wear the product."

She opened her mouth, then closed it again on a cautious sigh. "It's really a matter of viewpoint," she said carefully. "From yours, from de Marco's, even from the consumers', the clothes are the product. From the viewpoints of your producer, your director, your cinematographer and so forth, you're as much the product as the clothes you wear because we have to see that both of you are salable. If I can't make you look good, what you're wearing might as well be flea market special."

He saw the logic but didn't care for it. "I won't be a commodity."

"Parks, you're a commodity every time you walk out on the diamond. This really isn't any different." Exasperated, she lifted her hands palms up. "You sell tickets to Kings games, baseball cards and fielder's caps. Don't be so damned sanctimonious about this."

"First it's temperamental, now it's sanctimonious," he muttered disgustedly. "I suppose what it comes down to is we look at this little . . . venture from two different perspectives."

Brooke felt a light flutter of fear inside her breast. "I told you," she said quietly, "that it would be difficult."

His eyes came back to her, recognizing the shield she was already prepared to bring down. Parks ran a finger down her cheek. "And I told you it would be fun."

Leaning closer, he brushed his lips over hers. "We're both right. I have some things to do. Can I meet you back here later?"

Relaxing, Brooke told herself she had imagined the fear. "If you like. I'll probably be tied up until around five."

"Fine. You can cook me that dinner you promised me last night."

Brooke lifted her chin. "I never promised to cook you dinner," she corrected. "But perhaps I will."

"I'll buy the wine." Parks sent her a grin before he turned away.

"Wait." After a moment, Brooke went after him. "You don't have your car."

Parks shrugged. "I'll take a cab." He saw her hesitate then struggle with a decision.

"No," she said abruptly, digging in her bag. "You can use mine."

Parks took the keys, and her hand. He knew enough about her to realize offering the use of her car, or anything else important to her, wasn't a casual gesture. "Thank you."

Her color rose—the first truly self-conscious thing he had noticed about her. "You're welcome." Quickly, she drew her hand from his and turned away. "See you at five," she called over her shoulder without stopping.

Brooke felt a bit foolish as she rode the elevator to Claire's office. How could she have blushed over a simple thank-you for the loan of a car? She glanced up at the numbers flashing over the elevator door. Oh, he knew her too well, she realized, knew her too well when she'd hardly told him anything.

He didn't know she still had the copy of *Little Women*

her second foster mother had given her. He didn't know that she had adored those temporary parents and had been devastated when a broken marriage had caused her to be placed in another foster home. He didn't know about the horrid little girl she had shared a room with during what she still considered the worst year of her life. Or the Richardsons, who had treated her more like a hired hand than a foster child. Or Clark.

With a sigh, Brooke rubbed her fingers over her forehead. She didn't like to remember—didn't like knowing that her growing feelings for Parks seemed to force her to face the past again. Oh, the hell with it, Brooke thought with a shake of her head. It *was* the past. And she was going to have enough trouble dealing with the present to dwell on it.

Steadier, she stepped out into the wide, carpeted corridor of Claire's floor. The receptionist, a pretty girl with lots of large healthy teeth, straightened in her chair at Brooke's approach. She'd worked on the top floor for over two years and was still more in awe of Brooke than of Claire.

"Good afternoon, Ms. Gordon."

"Hello, Sheila, Ms. Thorton's expecting me."

"Yes, ma'am." Sheila wouldn't have contradicted her if her life had depended on it.

Unaware of the impression she made, Brooke strode easily down the corridor and through a set of wide glass doors. Here, two secretaries, known as the twins only because of identical desks, labored away on word processors. The outer office was huge, scrupulously modern and cathedral quiet.

"Ms. Gordon." The first twin beamed a smile while the second one reached for the button on her intercom.

"She's expecting me," Brooke said simply and breezed by them into Claire's office. The door opened silently. Brooke was halfway across the pewter-colored carpet before she realized Claire was sound asleep at her desk. Totally stunned, Brooke stopped dead in her tracks and stared.

The chair Claire sat in was high-backed pale-gray leather. Her desk was ebony, gleaming beneath stacks of neat papers. The glasses Claire wore for reading were held loosely in her hand. A Chinese "literary painting" in color wash and ink hung on the wall to her right, while behind her L.A. sunshine poured through a plate-glass window. Unsure what to do, Brooke considered leaving as quietly as she had come, then decided it was best to stay. Walking to the squashy leather chair facing the desk, she sat, then gently cleared her throat. Claire's eyes snapped open.

"Morning," Brooke said brightly and grinned at Claire's uncharacteristic confusion. "You'd do better on the sofa if you want a nap."

"Just resting my eyes."

"Mm-hmm."

Ignoring the comment, Claire reached for the papers she had been reading before fatigue had won. "I wanted you to have a look at the script for the next de Marco spot."

"Okay." Brooke accepted the script automatically. "Claire, are you all right?"

"Don't I look all right?" she retorted.

Deciding to take her literally, Brooke studied her. Except for the heavy eyes, she decided, Claire looked better than ever. Almost, Brooke mused, glowing. "You look marvelous."

"Well then." Claire smoothed her hair before she folded her hands.

"Didn't you sleep well last night?" Brooke persisted.

"As it happens, I was out late. Now the script."

"With Lee Dutton?" The thought went through her mind and out her lips before she could stop it. Claire gave her a tolerant smile.

"As a matter of fact, yes."

Brooke set the script back on the desk. "Claire," she began, only to be interrupted by a knock on the door.

"Your lunch, Ms. Thorton." A tray was wheeled in by twin number one.

The scent of hot roast beef had Brooke rising. "Claire, I misjudged you." Lifting the cover from a hot plate, she inhaled. "Forgive me."

"Did you think I'd let you go hungry?" With a chuckle, Claire stood to move to the sofa. "Brooke, dear, I've known you too long. Bring me my salad and coffee like a good girl."

Nibbling on a potato wedge, Brooke obeyed. "Claire, I really want to talk with you about Lee Dutton."

"Of course." Claire speared a radish slice. "Sit down and eat, Brooke, pacing's bad for my digestion."

Plate in hand, Brooke approached the couch. She set it on the low coffee table, picked up half a roast beef sandwich and began. "Claire, are you actually dating Lee Dutton?"

"Does dating seem inappropriate to you for someone of my age, Brooke? Pass me that salt."

"No!" Flustered, Brooke looked down at Claire's outstretched hand. She gave her the salt shaker then took a defiant bite of her sandwich. "Don't be ridiculous," she muttered over it. "I can see you dating all manner of fabulous men. I have trouble seeing you out on the town with Lee Dutton.''

"Why?"

Brooke shifted her shoulders uncomfortably. This wasn't how she had intended it to go. "Well, he's nice enough, and certainly sharp, but he seems sort of . . . well." Brooke sighed and tried again. "Let's put it this way: I can see Lee Dutton in the neighborhood bowling alley. I can't picture you there."

"No. . . ." Claire pursed her lips in thought. "We haven't tried that yet."

"Claire!" Exasperated, Brooke rose and began to pace again. "I'm not getting through to you. Look, I don't want to interfere with your life—"

"No?" The mild smile had Brooke flopping back down on the couch.

"You matter to me."

Claire reached over to squeeze her hand. "I appreciate that. Brooke, I've been taking care of myself for a long time. I've even handled a few men."

A bit reassured, Brooke began to eat again. "I suppose if I thought you were really getting involved . . ."

"What makes you think I'm not?" At Brooke's gaping stare, Claire laughed.

"Claire, are you—are you . . ." She gestured, not quite certain she should put her thoughts into words.

"Sleeping with him?" Claire finished in her calm, cultured voice. "Not yet."

"Not yet," Brooke echoed numbly.

"Well, he hasn't asked me to." Claire took another bite of salad and chewed thoughtfully. "I thought he would by now, but he's quite conservative. Very sweet and old-fashioned. That's part of his appeal for me. He makes me feel very feminine. You can lose that at times in this business.''

"Yes, I know.'' Brooke picked up her iced tea and stared into it. "Do you—are you in love with him?''

"I think I am.'' Claire settled back against the gray-and-rose patterned sofa. "I was only in love once before, really in love. I was your age, perhaps a bit younger.'' Her smile was soft for a moment, a girl's smile. "In all the years in between, I've never met anyone I was attracted to enough, comfortable enough with, trusted enough, to think of marrying.''

Brooke took a long swallow of tea. She thought she understood Claire's phrasing all too well. "You're thinking of marriage?''

"I'm thinking I'm almost fifty years old. I've built this up''—she gestured to indicate Thorton—"I have a comfortable home, a nice circle of friends and acquaintances, enough new challenges to keep me from dying of boredom, and suddenly I've found a man who makes me want to curl up in front of a fire after a long day.'' She smiled slowly and rather beautifully—not the girl's smile this time. "It's a good feeling.'' She let her eyes slide to Brooke, who was watching her closely. "I'd hate to see you have to wait twenty more years for it. Parks is a great deal more than mildly attracted to you.''

For the third time, Brooke rose to pace the room. "We haven't known each other long,'' she began.

"You're a woman who knows her own mind, Brooke.''

"Am I?'' With a mordant smile, she turned

back. "Perhaps I do know how I think, how I feel. I don't really know Parks, though. What if I give too much? What's to stop him from getting bored and moving on?"

Claire met her eyes steadily. "Don't compare him, Brooke. Don't make him pass tests for all those old hurts."

"Oh, Claire." Passing a hand through her hair, Brooke walked to stare out of the window. "That's the last thing I want to do."

"What's the first thing?"

"It's always been to have my own. To have my own so that nobody can come along and say, 'Whoops, you really only borrowed this, time to give it back.'" She laughed a little. "Silly, I suppose I've never really shaken that."

"And why should you?" Claire demanded. "We all want our own. And to get it, you and I both know there are a few basic risks involved."

"I'm afraid I'm falling in love with him," Brooke said quietly. "And the closer I get, the more afraid I am that it's all going to crumble under my feet. I have a feeling I need this defense . . . that if I fall in love with him, I need this edge of control, this little pocket of power, to keep myself from getting demolished. Is that crazy?"

"No. You're not the kind of woman who gives herself completely without asking for something back. You did that once, but you were a child. You're a woman who needs a strong man, Brooke. One strong enough to take, strong enough not to take all." She smiled as Brooke turned to face her. "Give yourself a little time,'' she advised. ''Things have a way of falling into place.''

''Do they?''

Claire's smile widened. ''Sometimes it only takes twenty years.''

With a laugh, Brooke walked back to the sofa. ''Thanks a lot.''

Chapter 8

BROOKE SAT CROSS-LEGGED ON THE SOFTLY FADED
Oriental rug in Claire's den. Sometime during the fourth
inning she'd given up trying to sit in a chair. To her
right, Lee and Claire sat on a two-cushioned brocade
sofa. Billings had outdone herself by preparing her
specialty, Beef Wellington, then had been mutely offended when Brooke had done little more than shift the
food around on her plate. Though she chided herself for
being nervous, Brooke had been able to do nothing but
worry about the outcome of the play-offs since Parks had
taken off for the Valiants' home stadium.

She'd been able to catch part of the first afternoon
game on her car radio as she had driven to a location
shoot. One of the production crew had thought ahead,
bringing a portable radio with an earplug, and had kept
up a running commentary between takes. Brooke had
felt overwhelming relief when the Kings had taken the

first game, then frustration and more nerves when they had lost the second. Now, she watched the third on the television set in Claire's small, elegant den.

"That man was out at second," Brooke fumed, wriggling impotently on the faded royal-blue rug. "Anyone with two working eyes could see that."

As she launched her personal attack, the Kings' manager, a squat man with the face of a dyspeptic elf, argued with the second base umpire. If she hadn't been quite so furious herself, Brooke might have admired the manager's theatrical gestures as he spun around, rolled his eyes to heaven and pointed an accusing finger in the umpire's face. The umpire remained unmoved and the call stood. With the Kings holding on to a thin one-run lead, a runner on second with one out boded ill.

When the next batter sent one sailing over the fence and the slim lead changed hands, Brooke groaned. "I can't stand it," she decided, pounding her fists on the rug. "I just can't stand it."

"Brooke's become involved in the game," Claire murmured to Lee.

"So I've noticed." He dropped a light kiss on her cheek. "You smell wonderful."

The sensation of blood rising to her cheeks was pleasant. She had been romanced by suave masters of the game in the more than twenty-five years of her womanhood, but she couldn't remember one who had made her feel quite the way Lee Dutton could. If they had been alone, she would have snuggled closer, but remembering Brooke, she merely squeezed his hand. "Have some wine, dear," she said to Brooke as she reached for the iced bottle beside her. "Good for the nerves."

Because she was breathing a sigh of relief as the next

batter struck out, Brooke didn't acknowledge the teasing tone. "That's three out," she said as she took the cool glass from Claire.

"Two," Lee corrected.

"Only if you believe a nearsighted umpire," she countered, sipping. When he chuckled, she sent a grin over her shoulder. "At least I didn't call him a bum."

"Give yourself a little time," Lee advised, winking at Claire as she handed him a glass.

"You know, some of the players—" Brooke began, then broke off with a gasp as a smoking line drive was hit toward third. Her stomach muscles knotted instantly. Parks dove sideways, stretching his arm out toward the speeding ball. He nabbed it in the tip of his glove just before the length of his body connected with the hard Astroturf. Brooke thought she could feel the bone-rattling jolt herself.

"He got it!" Lee broke out of his casual pose with a jerk that nearly upset Claire's wine. "Look at that, look at that! He got it!" he repeated, pointing at the television image of Parks holding up the glove to show the catch while he still lay prone. "That young sonofa—" He caught himself, barely, and cleared his throat. "Parks is the best with a glove in the league," he decided. "In *both* leagues!" He leaned forward to pound Brooke companionably on the back. "Parks robbed him, kid. Stole a base hit from him as sure as God made little green apples."

Because she watched Parks stand up and brush himself off, Brooke relaxed. "I want to see it on replay," she murmured. "Slow motion."

"You'll see that play a dozen times before the night's through," Lee predicted. "And again on the eleven o'clock news. Hey, lookie here.'' Grinning, he gestured to the set. "That's what I call classy timing.''

Brooke shifted her concentration to the de Marco commercial. Of course she'd seen it a dozen times in the editing room, and again on television, but each time she watched, she searched for flaws. She studied the graphics as Parks's cool clear voice spoke out to her. "It's perfect,'' she said with a smile. "Absolutely perfect.''

"How's the next one coming?'' Lee asked Claire.

"It's just waiting for Parks to be available. We hope to shoot next week.''

He settled back again, one arm around Claire. "I'm going to enjoy seeing that one play during the series.''

"They still have two games to win,'' Brooke reminded him. "They're a run behind in this one, and—''

"The opera's not over till the fat lady sings,'' Lee said mildly.

Brooke swiveled her head to look at him. Claire was snug beside him, a crystal glass in one hand. Lee's paunch strained against the buttons of his checked shirt. The ankle of one leg rested on the knee of the other while his foot bounced up and down to some personal tune. Abruptly, Brooke saw them as a perfect match. "I like you, Lee,'' she said with a wide smile. "I really like you.''

He blinked twice, then his lips curved hesitantly. "Well, thanks, kid.''

She's just given us her blessing, Claire thought with an inward chuckle as she took Lee's hand in hers.

Brooke made her way through the airport crowd with steady determination. In addition to the usual flow of traffic at LAX, there were fans, mobs of fans, waiting to greet the incoming Kings team. Some carried handmade signs, others banners. There were, she noted with some amusement, a good number of truants in the Los Angeles school system that morning, not to mention a deficit in the work force. After the twelve-inning victory, Brooke thought the players deserved a bit of adulation. She also wondered if she'd ever be able to fight her way through so that Parks would see her. The impulse to surprise him, she realized, had not been practical. A truant father hoisted a truant second-grader onto his shoulders. Brooke grinned. Maybe not practical, but it was going to be fun.

Pushing her sunglasses atop her head, Brooke narrowed her eyes against the sun and waited for the plane to touch down. As it stopped being a dot in the sky and took on form, she began to experience the first flicker of nerves. She fidgeted nervously with her bag while she stood, crushed shoulder to shoulder, with excited fans.

He'll be tired, she thought as dozens of conversations buzzed around her. He's probably looking forward to going home and sleeping for twenty-four hours. Brooke ran a hand through her hair. I should have told him I was coming. She shifted her weight to the other foot, curled her fingers around the chain link in front of her and watched the plane glide to a stop.

The moment the door opened, the cheering started, building, rising as the first men began to deplane. They waved back, looking tired and somehow vulnerable without their uniforms. Men, she thought. Simply men suffering from jet lag and perhaps a few hangovers. Then she smiled, deciding that the gladiators might have looked precisely the same the day after a bout.

As soon as she saw him, she felt warm. Beside

Brooke, a teenager grabbed her companion and squealed.

"Oh, there's Parks Jones! He's bee-utiful."

Brooke swallowed a laugh as she thought of how Parks would react to the adjective.

"Every time I watch him, my knees get weak." The teenager pressed her lithe young body against the fence. "Did you see him in that commercial? When he smiled, it was like he was looking right *at* me. I nearly died."

Though she didn't take her eyes off Parks, Brooke smiled inwardly. My plan exactly, she thought, pleased with herself. Tell your boyfriend to buy de Marco jeans. Then the sun fell on his hair and she found herself nearly as weak-limbed as the teenager. It's only been four days, she told herself. Why do I feel like a woman watching her man come home from the wars?

Though her sharp director's eye had seen a group of tense and tired men, the fans saw heroes. They cheered them. Some of the players merely waved and moved on, but most came up to the fence to exchange words, jokes, a touch of hands. Brooke watched Parks walk toward the barrier with a man she recognized as Snyder, the first baseman. She wondered, by the intensity of their discussion, if they were outlining infield strategy.

"It would only take twenty-five or thirty cans of shaving cream to fill his locker," Snyder insisted.

"Takes too long and evaporates too fast," Parks commented. "You've got to be practical, George."

Snyder swore mildly and lifted his hand in acknowledgment to a shout in the crowd. "Got a better idea?"

"Carbon dioxide." Parks scanned the crowd as they neared it. "Quick and efficient."

"Hey, yeah!" Pleased, Snyder gave him a slap on the back. "Knew your brains were good for something, Einstein."

"And as long as I help you work out the mechanics," Parks added, "my locker doesn't get filled with the thinking man's shaving cream."

"There's that, too," Snyder agreed. "Would you look at these people?" His grin widened. "Fantastic."

Parks started to agree, then spotted a mass of red hair touched with gold in the sunlight. The fatigue drained as though someone had pulled a cork. "Fantastic," he murmured and walked straight toward Brooke.

The teenager beside her made a moaning, melting sound and took a death grip on her friend's arm. "He's coming over here," she managed in a choked whisper. "Right over here. I know I'm going to die."

Brooke tilted her chin up so that her eyes would stay level with his as he stopped on the other side of the fence. "Hi." Parks's hand closed over hers on the metal wire. The simple contact was as intimate as anything she had ever known.

"Hi." Brooke smiled slowly, accepting the flare of desire and the sense of closeness without question.

"Can I get a lift?"

"Anytime."

He pressed his lips to the fingers still curled around the wire. "Meet me inside? I have to get my baggage."

Out of the corner of her eye, Brooke saw the two teenage girls gawking. "Great catch last night."

He grinned before he stepped away. "Thanks."

Snyder caught him by the arm as Brooke melted back into the crowd. "Hey, I like that catch better."

"Off limits," Parks said simply, making his way down the line of fans and outstretched hands.

"Aw, come on, Parks, we're teammates. All for one and one for all."

"Forget it."

"The trouble with Parks," Snyder began to tell a grandfatherly type behind the fence, "is he's selfish. I make his throws look good. I bite the bullet when he lines a hospital pitch at me. And what thanks do I get?" He sent Parks a hopeful smile. "You could at least introduce me."

Parks grinned as he signed a snatch of paper a fan thrust through a hole in the fence. "Nope."

It took him nearly thirty minutes to get away from the crowd and through the terminal. Impatience was growing in him. The simple touch of fingers outside had whetted his appetite for a great deal more. He'd never been lonely on the road before. Even if there was a rain out or an off day away from home, you were surrounded by people you knew. You became as close as a family—close enough to spend endless evenings together or opt to spend one alone without bruising feelings. No, he'd never been lonely. Until this time.

Parks couldn't count the times he had thought of her over the last four days, but he knew that everything had suddenly slipped back into focus the moment he had seen her standing there. Now he saw her again.

Brooke leaned back against a pillar near the baggage belt, Parks's suitcase at her feet. She smiled but didn't straighten as she saw him. She'd hate to have him know just how crazily her pulse was racing. "You travel light," she commented.

He cupped her face in his hand and, oblivious to the people milling around them, brought her close for a long, hard kiss.

"I missed you," he murmured against her mouth, then kissed her again.

There were enough of his teammates still loitering around to start up a chorus of approval.

"Excuse me." Snyder tapped Parks on the shoulder and grinned engagingly at Brooke. "I believe you've made a mistake. *I'm* George Snyder. This is our aging bat boy." He gave Parks an affectionate pat.

"How do you do." Brooke extended her hand and had it enveloped in a huge, hard palm. "Too bad about those two strikeouts last night."

There were several jeers as Snyder winced. "Actually, I'm luring the Valiants into complacency."

"Oh." Amused, Brooke gave him a big smile. "You did very well."

"Sorry, Snyder, time for your shot." Parks signaled to two teammates, who agreeably hooked their arms through Snyder's to haul him away.

"Aw, come on, Jones, give me a break!" Good-naturedly, Snyder let himself be dragged away. "I just want to discuss my strategy with her."

"Good-bye, George." Brooke waved as Parks bent to retrieve his bag.

"Let's get out of here."

With her fingers laced through his, Brooke had no choice but to follow. "Parks, you might have introduced me to your friends."

"Dangerous men," he stated. "All dangerous men."

With a chuckle, she matched her pace to his. "Yes, I

could see that. Especially the one holding a toddler on each hip.''

''There are a few exceptions.''

''Are you one?''

Parks caught her around the waist and drew her close against him. ''Uh-uh.''

''Oh, good. Want to come home with me and tell me your strategy?''

''That's the best offer I've had today.'' After tossing his bag in the rear of her car, Parks sprawled in the passenger seat. Accustomed to her driving pattern now, he relaxed and began to unwind by rambling about the previous day's game. Brooke said little, pleased to listen, glad that she had arranged to take the day off so that they could have a few hours together, alone.

''The commercial aired during each play-off game, you know,'' she commented as they headed out of town.

''How'd it look?'' Parks laid his head back against the seat. God, it was good to know he didn't have to go anywhere or do anything for twenty-four hours.

''Fantastic.'' As the road opened up, so did the Datsun's throttle. ''And I have it from the source that it plays very well.''

''Hmm?''

''A teenage girl in that mob today.'' With near perfect mimicry, Brooke related the girl's comments. She caught Parks's automatic grimace at the term *bee-utiful*, but swallowed a chuckle as she continued.

''Nice to know I devastate sixteen-year-old girls,'' he said dryly.

''You'd be surprised at the buying power of sixteen-year-old girls.'' With experienced ease, Brooke negotiated the curves on the narrowing road. "Not so much directly, certainly, but indirectly through their parents. And since they'd like their teenage boyfriends to make their knees weaken, too, they'll push them toward de Marco jeans, shirts, belts, *ad infinitum*." Tossing her hair back, she slid her eyes to his. "And you do have a great smile."

"Yeah." He gave a modest sigh. "I do."

Brooke stopped in her driveway with a deliberate jerk that had him swearing. Wisely slipping from the car before he could retaliate, she headed up the path.

"Just for that," Parks began as he dragged his bag out of the back, "I'm not going to give you the present I bought you."

At the door, Brooke turned, her grin changing to a look of bewilderment. "You bought me a present?"

Because she looked like a child who expected to be handed a brightly wrapped empty box, Parks treated it lightly. "I did. But I'm seriously considering keeping it myself now."

"What is it?"

"Are you going to open the door?"

Brooke shrugged, trying to pretend indifference as she turned the key. "There's a fire laid," she said as she breezed inside. "Why don't you light it while I get us some coffee?"

"Okay." Setting his bag down, Parks stretched travel-cramped muscles. With a wince, he pressed his fingers to the ribs still sore from their contact with Astroturf.

She'd brought some of her garden inside, he noted, spotting the bowl of vibrant mums and zinnias on the side table across the room. The table, he observed, was

Queen Anne; the bowl, dimestore special. Grinning, he went to the hearth. The combination suited her—the exquisite and the practical.

Parks struck a match and set it to the carefully rolled paper beneath the kindling. Dry wood caught with a crackle and a *whoosh*. He inhaled the smell that brought back flickering images of the past; evenings in the cozy parlor of his family home, camping trips with his uncle and cousins, weekends in England at the home of a college friend. He wanted to add to the pictures now with the memory of Brooke lying in his arms in front of the simmering fire while they made slow, endless love.

When he heard her returning, Parks stood, turning to face her as she entered with a tray holding a bottle and two glasses. "I thought you might want wine instead."

Smiling, Parks took the tray from her. "Yes." After setting the tray on the hassock, Parks lifted the bottle, examining the label with a lifted brow. "Is this a celebration?"

"A precelebration," Brooke countered. "I expect you to win tomorrow." She picked up both glasses, holding them out. "And if you don't, we'll have had the wine in any case."

"Seems fair." Parks poured pale-gold liquid into the stemmed glasses. Taking one from her, he clinked the rims together. "To the game?" he asked with a slow smile.

Brooke felt the quick nervous flutter in her stomach and nodded. "To the game," she agreed and drank. Her eyes widened but remained steady when he reached out to take a handful of her hair.

"I saw this in the sunlight," he murmured. "Even in

that mob of people at the airport, I'm not sure what I would have done if that fence hadn't been in the way." He let it sift through his fingers. "It was a long four days, Brooke."

She nodded, taking his hand to draw him onto the sofa beside her. The curves of her body seemed to fit naturally against the lines of his. "You're tense," she said quietly.

"Postseason games." He drew her closer, knowing the nerves would gradually drain before they built again the next day. "Maybe the lucky ones are the players raking leaves in their backyards in October."

"But you don't really think so."

Parks laughed. "No, I don't really think so. The play-offs pump you up until you're ready to explode, but the series . . ." He trailed off with a shake of his head. He didn't want to let his mind run that far ahead. The rules were three out of five—they weren't there yet. For now he didn't want to think of it, but of the woman beside him, the quiet afternoon and the long evening ahead. He thought that he'd remember her this way, a little pensive, with the smell of woodsmoke and fall flowers mixing with her own perfume. His mind drifted lazily, comfortably, as he sipped the iced wine and watched the flames dance.

"Have you been busy?"

Brooke tilted her head in absent agreement. She didn't want to think of work any more than Parks did. "The usual," she said vaguely. "E. J. talked me into seeing a perfectly dreadful movie where the cast pranced around in mythological costumes and shot lightning bolts."

"*Olympian Revenge?*"

"It had a talking three-headed dragon."

"That's the one. I caught it in Philadelphia last month when we had a rain out."

"I saw the mike in the frame three times."

Parks chuckled at her professional disdain. "Nobody else did," he assured her. "They were all asleep."

"Gross ineptitude keeps me awake." She leaned her head against his shoulder. It occurred to her how empty her home had been for the last few days, and how cozy it felt again. Brooke had never felt the need to share it before. In fact, she had always had a strong proprietary feeling about what was hers. Now, sitting quietly on the sofa, she realized she had already begun to give up her privacy, willingly and with total unawareness. Turning her head, she studied Parks's profile. "I missed you," she said at length.

He turned his head as well so that their lips were close, not quite touching. "I'd hoped you would." Then he shifted so that his mouth grazed her cheek. She trembled. Not yet, he told himself as the heat flared inside him. Not quite yet. "Maybe I'll give you that present after all."

Brooke's lips curved against his throat. "I don't believe you bought me anything at all."

Recognizing the ploy but willing to play, Parks rose. "You'll have to apologize for that," he said soberly as he walked to his suitcase. He flipped open the case then rummaged inside. When he stood again, Parks had a white box in his hands. Brooke regarded it curiously but with some of the wariness he had noted outside.

"What is it?"

"Open it and find out," he suggested, dropping it into her lap.

Brooke turned it over, examining the plain white box, testing it for weight. She wasn't a woman accustomed to spontaneous gifts and in the short time he had known her, Parks had already given her two. "You didn't have to—"

"You *have* to give your sister a Christmas present," he said mildly, sitting beside her again. "You're not my sister and it isn't Christmas."

Brooke frowned. "I'm not sure I understand the logic in that," she murmured then opened the lid. Packed in wads of tissue paper was a fat pink ceramic hippo with heavily lashed eyes, a flirtatious grin and varicolored polka dots. With a laugh, Brooke drew it out. "She's gorgeous!"

"She reminded me of you," Parks commented, pleased with the laugh and the look of humor in her eyes when she turned them to him.

"Is that so?" She held the hippo up again. "Well, she does have rather fetching eyes." Touched, she stroked the wide ceramic flank. "She really is sweet, Parks. What made you think of it?"

"I thought she'd fit into your menagerie." Seeing the puzzled look on her face, he gestured toward the shelf that held her monkey and bear. "Then there's that pig on the front door, the little carving of a jack rabbit in your bedroom, the china owl on the windowsill in the kitchen."

Comprehension came slowly. There were animals of varying types and materials scattered all through the house. She'd been collecting them for years without having the slightest idea what she was doing. But Parks had seen. Without an instant of warning to either of them, Brooke burst into tears.

Stunned, then alarmed, Parks reached for her, not having a clue what he would offer comfort for. Still, he'd seen enough tears from his sisters to know that logic often had nothing to do with tears. Ashamed, and unable to stem the flow, Brooke evaded his arms and rose. "No, no, please. Give me a minute. I *hate* to do this."

Even as he told himself to respect her wishes, Parks was going to her. Despite her resistance, he pulled her against him. "I can't stand to *see* you do it," he muttered; then, with a hint of exasperation, "Why are you doing it?"

"You'll think I'm stupid. I hate being stupid."

"Brooke." Firmly, he cupped a hand under her chin and lifted it. Tears rolled freely down her cheeks. Knowing no other remedy, he kissed her—the soft lips, the wet cheeks, the damp eyelids. What began as a blind effort to comfort grew to smoldering passion.

He could feel it build in him as his mouth sought hers again. His hands moved through her hair like those of a man making his tentative way through bolts of silk. She trembled against him—sobs or desire Parks was no longer sure as the kiss went deeper and deeper. She opened for him, more giving than he could remember. Her defenses were down, he reminded himself, fighting the impatience to fill his own needs quickly. His murmurs were quiet-pitched to soothe, his hands gently stroking to arouse.

Even recognizing her own vulnerability, Brooke didn't resist. She wanted to drift into that smoky, weightless world where every movement seemed to be in slow motion. She wanted to feel that fire and flash that left you breathless. She wanted the down-soft contentment that would lull you to sleep and linger in the morning.

As he lowered her to the floor, the scent of wood-smoke grew stronger. Brooke could hear the pop and hiss of the logs as flames ate at them. His long patient kisses held her suspended—half in the reality of the wool rug beneath her back, the red flickers of firelight and sun on her closed lids, half in the world of dreams lovers understand. While her mind floated, flirting with each separate sensation, he undressed her.

Parks took infinite care with the tiny round buttons of her blouse, as if he could wait until seasons changed outside the tall windows. There was no time here, no winter, no spring, only one everlasting moment. Brooke slipped her hands under his shirt, fingertips gliding over the warmth and the strength. As patient as he, she drew the material up, over his shoulders, then discarded it.

Flesh against flesh, they lay before the fire while the sun streamed through the massive windows and pooled over them. Kisses grew longer, interrupted only for sighs, for murmurs. She tasted the mellow warmth of wine on his tongue and was intoxicated.

Slowly, his mouth never leaving hers, Parks began to explore her body. Tiny, needlelike chills ran over her flesh, chasing the path of his hands. Feeling the light graze of his knuckles against the side of her breast, Brooke moaned, a liquid sound of pleasure. He took his tongue deeper into her mouth, gently exploiting this small weakness until the drug took full effect. She was limp, languid, utterly his. Then and only then did he give his lips the freedom to taste her skin again. It was as pungent as her scent, and somehow more erotic.

With moist, open-mouthed kisses he savored her, entranced her. Then the quick pressure of his teeth on some sensitive spot would bring her sharply aware, gasping with the change. His lips would soothe again, lulling her back into pliancy. Again and again he yanked her toward the flame, then guided her back to the clouds, until Brooke was no longer certain which she most desired.

She felt him draw her slacks down over her hips while he pressed those soul-wrenching kisses along her stomach. A mindless excitement filled her, rendering her helpless to do any more than move as he requested. His breath was warm on her intimate flesh so that the long muscles in her thighs trembled then went lax.

Still his mouth moved slowly. The hands that had already discovered every secret point of pleasure continued to caress and linger, keeping her trapped beneath a thin sheet of silken passion. The power she had experienced before moved through her, but her mind was too dazed to recognize it. She felt herself balanced on a slender edge—desire's tightrope—and wanted to continue to walk it as much as she longed to fall headlong into the wild, churning sea below. Then he was above her again, his eyes looking down into hers for a long, long, moment before his lips descended. He was waiting, and she understood. Their mouths still clinging, Brooke guided him inside her.

Her moan melted into his mouth, hot and passionate. Though she was clinging to him now with a sudden, fierce strength, Parks moved slowly. Brooke felt herself fill, fill to the desperate point of explosion. Then the shudders, wracking, convulsive, until she seemed to slide back down some smooth cool path to the torrent again. Like a swimmer trapped in rushing white water, she was swept from peak to peak while he moved with tortuous slowness. She could feel the tight, tense control in him, hear it in the quick labored breaths that merged with hers as he prolonged the pleasure, and the agony. Then he murmured something—a prayer, a plea, an oath—and took them both tumbling off the tightrope.

He must have slept. Parks thought he had closed his eyes for only an instant, but when he opened them again, the slant of the sun was different. Brooke was beside him, her hair wrapping them to each other. Her eyes were wide and aware as she stared into his. She'd been watching him for nearly an hour. Parks smiled and pressed his mouth to her shoulder.

"Sorry. Did I fall asleep?"

"For a little while." She hid her face against his neck a moment. It was as though he had stripped off her flesh, exposing all her thoughts. She wasn't quite certain what she should do about it. "You must have been exhausted."

"Not anymore," he said truthfully. He felt alert, pumped with energy and . . . clean. The last made him give a quick shake of his head. He stroked a hand down her arm. "There was something I wanted to ask you before I got . . . distracted." Propping himself on his elbow, Parks looked down at her. "Why were you crying?"

Brooke moved her shoulders in a shrug and started to shift away. With a firm hand, Parks stopped her. He could feel the effort she was making to draw back from him, but he realized he could no longer permit it. Whether she knew it or not, she had given herself to him completely. He was going to hold her to it.

"Brooke, don't try to block me out," he said quietly. "It won't work anymore."

She started to protest, but the quiet, steady look in his eyes told her he spoke nothing less than the truth. That alone should have been a warning of where her heart was taking her. "It was a sweet thing to do," she said at length. "I'm not used to sweetness."

Parks lifted a brow. "That's part of it, perhaps. What's the rest?"

With a sigh, Brooke sat up. This time he let her. "I hadn't realized I'd been collecting." With both hands, she pushed her hair back, then wrapped her arms around her knees. "I overreacted when you pointed it out. I always wanted a dog, a cat, a bird, anything when I was growing up. It wasn't feasible the way I shifted around." She moved her shoulders again, causing her tumbled hair to shiver over her naked back. "It was kind of shattering to realize I was still compensating."

Parks felt a chord of sympathy and suppressed it. There was no quicker way to alienate her. "You've got your own home, your own life now. You could have anything you wanted." Reaching around her, he poured more wine for both of them. "You don't have to compensate." He sipped, studying her profile.

"No," she agreed in a murmur. "No, I don't."

"What kind of dog do you want?"

Brooke twirled the glass in her hand, then suddenly laughed. "Something homely," she said, turning to grin at him. "Something down-to-the-ground homely." She reached out, laying a hand on his cheek. "I didn't even thank you."

Parks considered, nodding solemnly as he took the glass from her hand. "No, you didn't." In a quick move, he had her rolling on top of him. "Why don't you thank me now?"

Chapter 9

CLAIRE CAME DOWN TO GIVE THE SET HER FINAL approval. At the far end of the studio, serenely indifferent to the piles of equipment, lights and shades, was a cozy living room scene. A deep, cushy sofa in shades of masculine brown was spotlighted as technicians made adjustments. On a table beside it was a Tiffany lamp which would appear to give the soft, sexy lighting the crew was working to achieve. Claire worked her way around cable and cases to a new angle.

Tasteful, she decided. And effective. De Marco was pleased with the first spot. So pleased, Claire thought with a mild grimace, that he had insisted his current inamorata appear in this one. Well, that was show business, she decided as she checked her watch. Brooke had moaned and groaned at the casting, then had given in with the mutter that at least he hadn't insisted they write her any dialogue.

The studio segment was being filmed first, though it would appear at the end of the ad when aired. Judging Parks's temperament, Brooke had decided to go with what would probably be the most difficult portion for him first, then ease him into the rest. And, Claire mused as she checked her watch, their luck was holding. The Kings would compete in the World Series the following week, giving the commercials just that much more impact.

Outside the studio, a long buffet had been set up in the hall. E. J., the production coordinator and the assistant cameraman were already making the most of it. Brooke was in the studio, nibbling on a hunk of cheese as she supervised the finer details.

"Damn it, Bigelow, that light's flickering again. Change the bulb or get a new fixture in here. Silbey, let me see what kind of effect we get with that new gel."

Obediently, he hit a switch so that the light filtered through the colored sheet and came out warm and sultry. "Okay, not bad. Sound?"

The sound technician walked under the boom mike. With her face innocently bland, she began to recite a nursery rhyme with a few interesting variations. At the polite volley of applause, she curtsied.

"Any problems?" Claire asked as she moved to stand beside Brooke.

"We've smoothed them out. Your end?"

"Everyone's accounted for. The talent's changing." Absently, she straightened the hem of her sleeve. "I got a glimpse of de Marco's lady. She's gorgeous."

"Thank God," Brooke said with feeling. "Are we expecting him?"

"No." Claire smiled at the resigned tone of Brooke's

voice. She heartily disliked relatives, friends or lovers hanging around a shoot. "He tells me Gina claims he would make her nervous, but he left no doubt she's to be given the royal, kid-glove treatment."

"I won't bite her," Brooke promised. "I ran through Parks's lines with him. He has it cold . . . if he doesn't fumble it on camera."

"He doesn't appear to be a fumbler."

Brooke smiled. "No. And I think he's starting to enjoy this whole business despite himself."

"Good. I have a script I want him to read." Above their heads on a ladder, someone cursed pungently. Claire's smooth features never registered she had even heard. "There's a part, a small one, I think he's perfect for."

Brooke turned to give Claire her full attention. "A feature?"

She nodded. "For cable. We won't be casting for another month or two, so he's got plenty of time to think about it. I'd like you to read it, too," she added casually.

"Sure." Mulling over the idea of Parks as an actor, Brooke turned to call out another instruction.

"You might like to direct it."

The order froze in her throat. "What?"

"I know you're happy directing commercials," Claire went on as if Brooke weren't gaping at her. "You've always said you enjoy creating the quick and intense, but this script might change your mind."

"Claire"—Brooke might have laughed if she hadn't been stunned—"I've never directed anything more complex than a sixty-second spot."

"Like the promo for the new fall shows you filmed

last summer? Three major network stars told me you were one of the best they'd ever worked with." It was said dryly, hardly like a compliment. "I've wanted to ease you into something like this for a long time, but I didn't want to push." Claire patted her hand. "I'm still not pushing, just read the script."

After a moment, Brooke nodded. "All right, I'll read it."

"Good girl. Ah, there's Parks now." Her eyes ran over him with professional discrimination. "My, my," she murmured, "he does wear clothes well."

He looked as though he had chosen the pale-blue cashmere sweater and slate-gray jeans at random, shrugging into them without a thought. That they fit with tailored precision wasn't nearly as important as the sense of rightness—that careless style that comes not from money but from basic class.

That he had, Brooke thought. Beneath the attractive face and athletic body was a sense of class that one was born with or one was not. It could never be taught. He held a glass of ginger ale in his hand, looking over the rim as he studied the room.

He found it crowded and cluttered and apparently disorganized but for the small island of order that was a sofa, table and lamp. He wondered fleetingly how anyone could work sanely around the coiled snakes of cable, huge black cases and poles of lights. Then he saw Brooke. She could, he thought with a smile. She would simply steamroll over the chaos until she got exactly what she wanted. She might have wept like a child in his arms only a few nights before, but when she was on the job she was as tough as they came.

Perhaps, he mused, that was why he'd fallen in love with her—and perhaps that was why he was going to keep that little bit of information to himself for a while. If he'd nearly panicked when he'd realized it, Brooke would undoubtedly do so. She wasn't quite ready to sit trustingly in the palm of his hand.

Brooke moved toward him, eyes narrowed. Parks thought uncomfortably that she could always make him feel like a department store dummy when she looked at him that way. It was her director's look, appraising, searching for flaws, mulling over the angles.

"Well?" he said at length.

"You look marvelous." If she had noticed the faint irritation in his voice, she ignored it. Reaching up, she disheveled his hair a bit, then studied the effect. "Yes, very good. Nervous?"

"No."

Her face softened with a smile. "Don't frown, Parks, it won't help you get into the mood. Now . . ." Linking her arm in his, she began to lead him toward the set. "You know your lines, but we'll have cue cards in case you draw a blank, so there's nothing to worry about. The main thing we want is that sort of laid-back, understated machismo. Remember this is the end of the segment; the first scene you're on the field in uniform, then there's the business in the locker room while you're changing, then this. Soft lights, a little brandy, a beautiful woman."

"And I owe it all to de Marco," he said dryly.

"The woman in any case," she returned equably. "It's simply a statement that clothes suit a man's image. Hopefully, men will be convinced that de Marco's right for theirs. You'll sit here." Brooke gestured toward the end of the couch. "Give me that relaxed slouch of yours when you're unwinding. It's casual but not sloppy."

He frowned again, helplessly annoyed that she could dissect his every gesture and put a label on it. "Now?"

"Yes, please." Brooke stood back while Parks settled himself on the couch. "Yes, good. . . . Bring your elbow back just a bit on the arm. Okay." She smiled again. "That's what I want. You're getting very good at this, Parks."

"Thanks."

"You'll talk right into the camera this time," she told him, gesturing behind her to where the machine sat on a dolly. "Easy, relaxed. The girl will come up behind you, leaning over as she hands you the brandy snifter. Don't look at her, just touch her hand and keep talking. And smile," she added, looking at her watch. "Where is the girl?"

On cue, Gina entered, tall and voluptuous, followed by a stern-looking blonde and two men in business suits. Better than the photo de Marco had sent over, Brooke noted, and that had been impressive. The woman was young, but not too young, a ripe twenty-five, Brooke estimated, with large sloe eyes and raven hair. Her body was curvy, shown to advantage in a clingy low-cut gown that stopped just short of censorship. She wouldn't get aloof from this one, Brooke mused, watching Gina make her way across the studio. Heat vibrated in every movement. This time she would go for pure sex—for the five and a half seconds Gina was on screen. For a thirty-second television ad, it would be more than enough.

Ignoring the appreciative mutters and elbowing of her

crew, Brooke walked to meet de Marco's lady. "Hello." She extended her hand with a smile. "I'm Brooke Gordon, I'll be directing you."

"Gina Minianti," she purred in a voice that instantly made Brooke regret she'd have no lines.

"We're very pleased to have you, Ms. Minianti. Do you have any questions before we begin?"

Gina gave her a slight smile. *"Come?"*

"If there's anything you don't understand," Brooke began, only to have the blonde interrupt her.

"Signorina Minianti doesn't speak English, Ms. Gordon," she said briskly. "Weren't you informed?"

"Doesn't—" Breaking off, Brooke rolled her eyes to the ceiling. "Lovely."

"I'm Mr. de Marco's personal secretary. I'll be glad to translate."

Brooke gave the blonde a long hard look, then turned around. "Places," she called. "It's going to be a long day."

"A little stumbling block?" Parks murmured as she passed him.

"Shut up and sit down, Parks."

Controlling a grin, he stepped forward to take Gina's hand. "Signorina," he began, then caught Brooke's full attention when he continued in fluid Italian. Beaming, Gina answered in a rapid spate, gesturing freely with her other hand.

"She's excited," Parks commented, knowing Brooke had stopped in her tracks behind him.

"So I gathered."

"She's always wanted to do an American movie." He spoke to Gina again, something that made her throw back her magnificent head and laugh throatily. Turning, she dismissed the blonde with a flick of the wrist and tucked her arm through Parks's. When they faced her, the tawny Californian, the raven Italian, Brooke was struck with the perfection of contrast. That five and a half seconds of film, she thought, was going to crackle like a forest fire—and sell one hell of a lot of de Marco merchandise.

"You seem to speak Italian well enough to suit her," Brooke commented.

"Apparently." He grinned again, noting that Brooke wasn't the least jealous but appraising, as if he and Gina were already in a view screen. "She'd like me to interpret for her."

"All right, tell her we'll run through it once to show her what she needs to do. Let's have the lights!" Striding to the set, Brooke waited impatiently while Gina and Parks strolled behind her, heads close as he relayed Brooke's instructions. "Sit down, Parks, and tell her to watch closely. I'll run through it with you." Parks settled on the couch as she had instructed him. "Take it from the top, just as if the camera were rolling."

He began, talking easily, as if to a few friends on a visit. Perfect, Brooke thought as she picked up the prop brandy snifter and walked into camera range behind the couch. She leaned over, letting her cheek come close to his as she offered it. Without glancing from the camera, Parks accepted it, raising the fingers of his other hand to run down the back of Brooke's as it rested on his shoulder. She straightened slowly, moving out of camera range as he finished the dialogue.

"Now ask her if she understands what she's to do," Brooke ordered.

Gina lifted an elegant hand at Parks's question, silently communicating "of course."

"Let's try one." Brooke backed behind E. J. and the assistants who would dolly the camera platform forward for the close-ups. "Quiet on the set," she called, effectively cutting off a few discreet murmurs. "Roll film. . . ." The clapper struck—Parks Jones for de Marco, scene three, take one. She narrowed her eyes at Parks. "Action."

He ran through it well enough for a first take, but Brooke decided he hadn't warmed to it yet. Gina followed instructions, bringing the snifter, leaning over him suggestively. Then she glanced up, startled, as the camera rolled in.

"Cut. Parks, explain to Gina not to look at the camera, please." She smiled at the woman, hoping she communicated patience and understanding. She needed a great deal of both by the fifth take. Instead of becoming more used to the camera, Gina seemed to be growing more unnerved. "Five minutes," Brooke announced. The hot lights switched off, and the crew began a pilgrimage toward the buffet. With another smile, Brooke gestured for Gina to join her and Parks on the sofa. "Parks, will you tell her she need only be natural. She's gorgeous, the few seconds she's going to be on film will make a tremendous impact."

Gina listened with brows knit, then tossed Brooke a smile. *Gràtzie.*" Taking Parks's hand, she launched into a long, emotional torrent that turned out to be an apology for her clumsiness and a request for something cold to calm her nerves.

"Bring Signorina Minianti some orange juice,"

Brooke demanded. "Tell her she's not clumsy at all,'' Brooke continued diplomatically. "Ah, tell her to try to imagine you're lovers, and when the camera turns off—"

"I get the idea," Parks said with a grin. When he spoke to Gina again, she gave her throaty laugh then shook her head before she answered. "She says she'll try to imagine it," Parks relayed to Brooke, "but if she imagines it too well, Carlo will step on my face . . . or words to that effect."

"We have to sacrifice for our art," Brooke told him dryly. "Parks, it would help if you could put a little more steam into it."

"Steam?" he repeated, lifting a brow.

"A man who doesn't steam a bit with a woman like that hanging over his shoulder needs a transfusion." Rising, Brooke patted his shoulder. "See what you can do?"

"Anything for art," he returned, sending her a wolfish grin.

As E. J. sat behind his camera again, Brooke walked to stand at his shoulder. "Let's see if we can make one this time," she muttered.

"Boss, I can do this all day long." He focused his lens on Gina and sighed. "I think I've died and gone to heaven."

"De Marco might arrange it if you don't watch your step. Places!"

Better, she mused. Yes, definitely better as they completed the sixth take. But not perfect. She told Parks to ask Gina to give the camera a languid look before she slid Parks an under-the-lashes smile. The direction lost something in the interpretation. "Cut. Here, tell her to stand next to the camera and watch again." Brooke took Gina's place, moving behind him as he spoke, cupping the snifter of lukewarm tea. This time when Parks took it from her, he brought her other hand to his lips, pressing a soft kiss against it without breaking the rhythm of the dialogue. Brooke felt a jolt shoot up her arm and forgot to move away.

"Just seemed natural," Parks told her, linking his fingers through hers.

Brooke cleared her throat, aware that her crew was watching with avid interest. "Give it a try that way, then," she said matter-of-factly. She walked back to E. J., but when she turned, Parks's eyes were still on her. Brooke gave a quick, frustrated shake of her head. She knew that look. Slowly, the meaning crystal-clear, Parks smiled.

"Places!" Brooke called in her own defense.

It took three more takes before she got just what she wanted. A hot but self-satisfied Gina gave Parks two exuberant kisses, one on each cheek, then came over and chattered something at Brooke. Glancing up at Parks, Brooke saw that amused and all too innocent look on his face.

"Just say thank you," he advised.

"Thank you," Brooke said obediently as Gina took her hand and squeezed it. She swept off with her entourage. "What was I thanking her for?" Brooke used the sleeve of her shirt to dry the sweat on her forehead.

"She was complimenting your taste."

"Oh?"

"She said your lover was magnificent."

Dropping her arm, Brooke stared at him. "Really?" she said coolly.

Parks grinned, gave a deprecatory shrug then strolled off to see if anything was left at the buffet.

Hands on her hips, Brooke stared after him. She wouldn't give him the satisfaction of letting her own smile escape. "Location, one hour," she called out.

Brooke had been right in thinking that the third brief scene of the commercial would be the most difficult to film. She shot the second scene next, crowding lights, equipment and crew into the Kings locker room. Claire had arranged, with a little negotiating, to have a few of the better-known of Parks's teammates available for background or cameos. Once Brooke got them settled down so that they stopped waving at the camera or making fictitious announcements into the mike, it began to work. And work well.

Because of the relative ease with which the segment was progressing, Brooke found the headache growing at the base of her skull unexplainable. True, the locker room was noisy between takes, and after the first hour of many bodies under hot lights, it *smelled* like a locker room, but this headache was pure tension.

At first she simply ignored it; then, when that became impossible, she grew annoyed with herself. There was nothing to be tense about. Parks did what he was told, pulling the cashmere sweater over his naked chest for each take. And every time he smiled at her, Brooke felt the headache pulse.

By the time the crew was setting up for the scene on the diamond, Brooke had convinced herself she had it under control. It was just a nagging ache, something she would take care of with a couple of aspirin when she got home. As she watched the sound technician work on a mike, she felt a beefy arm slip over her shoulders.

"Hi." Snyder grinned down at her, drawing an automatic smile of response from Brooke. He was, she thought, about as dangerous as a cocker spaniel.

"Ready for the next scene, George? You did very well before. Of course, you won't be on camera this time."

"Yeah, I wanted to mention that you're making a big mistake using Parks. Too skinny." He flexed a well-muscled arm.

Brooke gave his biceps a nod of approval. "I'm afraid I don't have anything to do with the casting."

"Too bad. Hey, now that I'm a star, are you going to pick me up at the airport?"

"Forget it, Snyder." Before Brooke could answer, Kinjinsky strolled over, a bat in one hand, a ball in the other. "She's out of your league." He grinned at Brooke, jerking his head at his teammate. "He specializes in belly dancers."

"Lies." Snyder looked amazingly like an overgrown choirboy. "All lies."

"When my daughter grows up," Kinjinsky said mildly, "I'm going to warn her about men like him." Walking to the plate, he tossed the ball up in the air then drilled it out to center field.

"Kinjinsky's the best fungo hitter on the team," Snyder told Brooke. "Too bad he has such trouble with a pitched ball."

"At least I can make it from first to second in under two and a half minutes," Kinjinsky tossed back.

Snyder, well used to ribbing about his base running,

feigned an offended look. "I have this genetic anatomical problem," he explained to Brooke.

"Oh." Playing along, she looked sympathetic. "That's too bad."

"It's called a lead foot," Parks commented as he came up behind them.

Hearing his voice had the headache she'd nearly forgotten drumming again. She turned to find him watching her and his teammates with a lazily amused smile. Parks wore full uniform, the blazing white that brought out the gold of his skin. The navy cap shaded his eyes, giving him a cocky, assured look. Quietly possessive, his eyes skimmed over her. This time Brooke felt a flutter in her stomach in addition to the throb at the base of her neck.

"Just keeping your woman entertained," Snyder said genially.

"Brooke's her own woman." But there was something unmistakably proprietary in the disclaimer.

Hearing it, Snyder realized there was something deeper here than he had imagined. So the lightning's finally hit the Iceman, he thought. Snyder had the wit to rib unmercifully and the nature of a man who mends the broken wings of small birds. "When she sees how good I come across on camera, you're going to be out of a job."

"De Marco doesn't have a line for sumo wrestlers," Parks countered.

"Gentlemen." Brooke spoke, cutting them off. "The crew's ready. George, if you'd take your place at first to give Parks his target."

"Ouch." He winced. "Try not to take that literally, Jones. I don't want to be on the disabled list next week."

"Mike." Brooke stepped over to Kinjinsky. "If you'll just hit them to Parks—don't make it too easy for him, I want to see a little effort."

With a grin, Kinjinsky tossed up another ball. "I'll see what I can do."

Nodding, Brooke walked toward the crew. "Places. Parks, any questions?"

"I think I can handle this one." He stepped up to third, automatically kicking up a bit of dust with his spikes.

She looked through the lens, feeling another flutter in her stomach as she focused on Parks. Shifting his weight to one hip, he grinned at her. Brooke stepped back, gesturing to E. J.

"Hey, boss, you okay?"

"Yes, I'm fine. Roll film."

It went perfectly. Brooke knew she could have used the first take without a hitch, but opted for two more. They were equally smooth. Kinjinsky blasted the ball at Parks, enough to make him dive or leap before Parks in turn fired the ball at Snyder on first.

"Third take's the winner," E. J. announced when Brooke called the session a wrap.

"Yes." Unconsciously, she rubbed the back of her neck.

"He shouldn't have even caught it," E. J. went on, watching Brooke as he began to load his equipment.

"He seems to excel at doing the impossible," she murmured.

"Headache?"

"What?" Glancing down, she found E. J. watching her steadily. "It's nothing." Annoyed, she dropped her hand. Parks was already in a conference on the mound with his two teammates. He had his glove hand on his hip, grinning at Snyder's newest concept for a practical joke. "It's nothing," Brooke repeated in a mutter, reaching for one of the sodas in the ice chest.

It had to be nothing, she told herself as she tipped the bottle and drank deeply. Whatever was rolling around inside her was just a product of fatigue after a long day's work. She needed aspirin, a decent meal and eight hours' sleep. She needed to stay away from Parks.

The minute the thought entered her head, Brooke was infuriated. He has nothing to do with it, she told herself fiercely. I'm tired, I've been working too hard, I've— She caught E. J.'s speculative stare and bristled.

"Would you get out of here?"

His face cleared with a wide grin. "On my way. I'll drop off the film at editing."

With a curt nod, Brooke strode out to the mound to thank Snyder and Kinjinsky. She heard the tail of Snyder's brainstorm, something about frogs in the bullpen, before Parks turned to her.

"How'd it go?"

"Very well." Heat was running along her skin now, too physical, too tangible. She gave her attention to his teammates. "I want to thank both of you. Without your help, it never would have gone so smoothly."

Snyder leaned his elbow on Kinjinsky's shoulder. "Just keep me in mind when you want something more than a pretty face in one of these commercials."

"I'll do that, George."

Parks waited through the rest of the small talk, adding comments easily though his concentration was all for Brooke. He waited until the ball players had wandered off toward the locker room before he took Brooke's chin in his hand. Closely, patiently, he examined her. "What's wrong?"

Brooke stepped away so that they were no longer touching. "Why should anything be wrong?" she countered. Her nerves had gone off like bells in her head at his touch. "It went very well. I think you'll be pleased with it when it's edited. With the two spots running throughout the series, we won't shoot another until November." Turning, she noted that most of the crew had gone. She found she wanted to be away before she and Parks were completely alone. "I have a few things to clear up back at the office, so—"

"Brooke." Parks cut her off cleanly. "Why are you upset?"

"I'm *not* upset!" Biting back fury, she whirled back to him. "It's been a long day, I'm tired. That's all."

Slowly, Parks shook his head. "Try again."

"Leave me alone," she said in a trembling undertone that told her, and him, just how close she was to the edge. "Just leave me alone."

Dropping his mitt to the ground, he took both her arms. "Not a chance. We can talk here, or we can go back to your place and hash it out. Your choice."

She shoved away from him. "There's nothing to hash out."

"Fine. Then let's go have dinner and see a movie."

"I told you I had work to do."

"Yeah." He nodded slowly. "You lied."

Sharp, bubbling anger filled her eyes. "I don't have to lie, all I have to do is tell you no."

"True enough," he agreed, holding on to his own temper. "Why are you angry with me?" His voice was calm, patient. His eyes weren't. The sun fell against his face, accenting that fierce sexuality.

"I'm not angry with you!" she nearly shouted.

"People usually shout when they're angry."

"I'm *not* shouting," she claimed as her voice rose.

Curiously, he tilted his head. "No? Then what are you doing?"

"I'm afraid I'm falling in love with you." Her expression became almost comically surprised after the words had tumbled out. She stared in simple disbelief, then covered her mouth with her hand as if to shove the words back inside.

"Oh, yeah?" He didn't smile as he took another step toward her. Something was scrambling inside his stomach like a squirrel in a cage. "Is that so?"

"No, I . . ." In defense, she looked around, only to find that she was alone with him now. Alone in his territory. The stands rose up like walls to trap them inside the field of grass and dirt. Brooke backed off the mound. "I don't want to stay here."

Parks merely matched his steps to hers. "Why afraid, Brooke?" He lifted his hand to her cheek, causing her to stop her retreat. "Why should a woman like you be afraid of being in love?"

"I know what happens!" she said suddenly with eyes that were dark and stormy in contrast to the trembling tone.

"Okay, why don't you tell me?"

"I'll stop thinking, I'll stop being careful." She ran an agitated hand through her hair. "I'll give until I lose the edge, then when it's over I won't have anything left. Every time," she whispered, thinking of all the transient parents, thinking of Clark. "I won't let it happen to me again. I can't be involved with you for the fun of it, Parks. It just isn't working." Without being aware of the direction, Brooke had turned to pace to the third base bag. Parks felt the warmth of the gold piece against his chest and decided it was fate. Taking his time, he followed her. His percentage of errors at the corner was very small.

"You are involved with me, whether you're having fun at it or not."

She sent him a sharp glance. This wasn't the easy-going man but the warrior. Brooke straightened her shoulders. "That can be remedied."

"Try it," he challenged, calmly gripping her shirt in his hand and pulling her toward him.

Brooke threw her head back, infuriated, and perhaps more frightened than she had ever been in her life. "I won't see you again. If you can't work with me, take it up with Claire."

"Oh, I can work with you," he said softly. "I can even manage to take your orders without too much of a problem because you're damn good at what you do. I told you once before I'd follow your rules while the camera was on." He glanced around, silently relaying that there was no camera this time. "It's tough to beat a man on his own ground, Brooke, especially a man who's used to winning."

"I'm not a pennant, Parks," she said with amazing steadiness.

"No." With one hand still gripping her shirt, he traced the other gently down her cheek. "Pennants are won through teamwork. A woman's a one-on-one proposition. Seventh-inning stretch, Brooke. Time to take a quick breath before the game starts again.'' The hand on her cheek moved up to cup her neck. She wondered that he couldn't feel the sledgehammers pounding there. Then he smiled, that slow dangerous smile that always drew her. ''I'm in love with you.''

He said it so calmly, so simply, that it took her a moment to understand. Every muscle in her body went rigid. ''Don't.''

He lifted a brow. ''Don't love you or don't tell you?''

''Stop.'' She put both hands on his chest in an attempt to push him away. ''It's not a joke.''

''No, it's not. What are you more afraid of?'' he asked, studying her pale face. ''Loving or being loved?''

Brooke shook her head. She'd been so careful to keep from crossing that thin line—been just as careful to keep others from crossing from the other side. Claire had done it, and E. J., she realized. There was love there. But *in* love . . . How could a tiny, two-letter word petrify her?

''You could ask me when,'' Parks murmured, kneading the tense muscles in her neck, ''and I couldn't tell you. There wasn't a bolt of lightning, no bells, no violins. I can't even say it snuck up on me because I saw it coming. I didn't try to step out of the way.'' He shook his head before he lowered his mouth to hers. ''You can't wish it away, Brooke.''

The kiss rocked her back on her heels. It was hard and strong and demanding without the slightest hint of urgency. It was as if he knew she could go nowhere. She could fight him, Brooke thought. She could still fight him. But the tension was seeping out of her, filling her with a sense of freedom she had thought she would never fully achieve. She was loved.

Feeling the change in her, Parks pulled back. He

wouldn't win her with passion. His needs ran too deep to settle for that. Then her arms were around him, her cheek pressed against his chest in a gesture not of desire, but of trust. Perhaps the beginning of trust.

"Tell me again," she murmured. "Just tell me once more."

He held her close, stroking her hair while the breeze whispered through the empty stadium. "I love you."

With a sigh, Brooke stepped over the line. Lifting her head, she took his face in her hands. "I love you, Parks," she murmured before she urged his lips to take hers.

Chapter 10

CLUBHOUSES HAVE THEIR OWN SMELL. SWEAT, FOOT powder, the tang of liniments, the faint chemical aroma of whirlpools and the overlying fragrance of coffee. The mixture of odors was so much a part of his life, Parks never noticed it as he pulled on his sweat shirt. What he did notice was tension. That was inescapable. Even Snyder's determined foray of practical jokes couldn't break the curtain of nerves in the locker room that afternoon. When a team had spent months together—working, sweating, winning and losing—aiming toward one common goal, nothing could ease the nerves of facing the seventh game of the World Series.

If the momentum had been with them, the atmosphere would have been different. All the minor aches that plague the end of a season would barely have been noticed—the tired legs, the minor pulls. But the Kings had dropped the last two games to the Herons. A professional athlete knows that skill is not the only determining factor in winning. Momentum, luck, timing are all added for balance.

Even if the Kings could have claimed they'd fallen into a slump there might have been a little more cheer in the clubhouse. The simple fact was that they'd been outplayed. The number of hits between the opponents was almost even—but the Herons had made theirs count while the Kings had left their much needed runs stranded on base. Now it came down to the last chance for both teams. Then when it was over, they'd pick up their off-season lives.

Parks glanced at Snyder, who'd be on his charter boat in Florida the following week. Catching fish and swapping lies, he called it, Parks mused. Kinjinsky, getting heat applied to his ribs, would be playing winter ball in Puerto Rico. Maizor, the starting pitcher, would be getting ready to play daddy for the first time when his wife delivered in November. Some would go on the banquet circuit and the talk show circuit—depending on the outcome of today's game. Others would go back to quiet jobs until February and spring training.

And Parks Jones makes commercials, he reflected with a small grimace. But the idea didn't bring on the sense of foolishness it had only a few months before. It gave him a certain pleasure to act—though Brooke wouldn't call it that—in front of the camera. But he wasn't too thrilled with the poster deal Lee had cooked up.

He smiled a little as he drew on his spikes. Hype, Brooke had called it, saying simply it was part of the game. She was right, of course; she usually was about that aspect of things. But Parks didn't think he'd ever be completely comfortable with the way she could look him over with those calm eyes and sum him up with a few choice words. Wouldn't it disconcert any man to have fallen in love with a woman who could so accurately interpret his every expression, body move or careless word? Face it, Jones, he told himself, you could have picked an easier woman. Could have, he reflected, but didn't. And since Brooke Gordon was who and what he wanted, she was worth the effort it took to have her, and to keep her. He wasn't so complacent that he believed he had truly done either yet.

Yes, she loved him, but her trust was a very tenuous thing. He sensed that she waited for him to make a move so that she could make a countermove. And so the match continued. Fair enough, he decided; they were both programmed to compete. He didn't want to master her . . . did he? With a frown, Parks pulled a bat out of his locker and examined it carefully. If he had to answer the question honestly, he'd say he wasn't sure. She still challenged him—as she had from the very first moment. Now, mixed with the challenge were so many emotions it was difficult to separate them.

He'd been angry when Brooke wouldn't change her schedule and fly east during the games at the Herons' home stadium. And when he'd become angry, she'd become very cool. Her work, she had told him, couldn't be set aside to suit him or even herself . . . any more than his could. Even though he'd understood, Parks had been angry. He had simply wanted her there, wanted to know she was in the stands so that he could look up and see her. He had wanted to know she was there when the long game was over. Pure selfishness, he admitted. They both had an ample share of that.

With a grim smile Parks ran a hand down the smooth barrel of the bat. She'd told him it wouldn't be easy. Brooke had been her own person long before he had pushed his way into her life. Circumstances had made her the person she was—though they were circumstances she had still not made completely clear to him. Still it was that person—the strong, the vulnerable, the practical and the private—whom he had fallen for. Yet he couldn't quite get over the urge he had at times to shake her and tell her they were going to do it his way.

He supposed what epitomized their situation at this point was their living arrangement. He had all but moved in with her, though neither one of them had discussed it. But he knew Brooke considered the house hers. Therefore, Parks was living with her, but they weren't living together. He wasn't certain his patience would last long enough to break through that final thin wall—without leaving the entrance hole a bit jagged.

With a quiet oath he reached into the locker and grabbed a batting glove, sticking it in his back pocket. If he had to use a bit of dynamite, he decided, he would.

"Hey, Jones, infield practice."

"Yeah." He grabbed his mitt, sliding his hand into its familiar smoothness. He was going to handle Brooke, he told himself. But first there was a pennant to win.

Alternately cursing and drumming her fingers against the steering wheel, Brooke cruised the parking lot in search of a space. "I knew we should've left earlier," she muttered. "We'll be lucky to get anything within a mile of the stadium."

Leaning back against the seat, E. J. interrupted his

humming long enough to comment. "Still fifteen minutes before game time."

"When somebody gets you a free ticket," Brooke said precisely, "the least you can do is be ready when they pick you up. There's one!" Brooke gunned the motor and slipped between two parked cars with inches to spare. Hitting the brake, she glanced at her companion. "You can open your eyes now, E. J.," she said dryly.

Cautiously, one at a time, he did so. "Okay. . . ." He looked at the car beside him. "Now how do we get out?"

"Open the door and inhale," she advised, wiggling out her side. "And hurry up, will you? I don't want to miss them taking the field."

"I've noticed your interest in baseball's increased over the summer, boss." Thankful for his thin frame, E. J. squeezed out of the Datsun.

"It's an interesting game."

"Yeah?" Joining her, he grinned.

"Careful, E. J., I still have your ticket. I could scalp it twenty times before we reach the door."

"Aw, come on, Brooke, you can tell your friend what's already in the papers."

She scowled at that, stuffing her hands in her pockets. There'd been pictures of her and Parks, tantalizing little articles and hints in every paper she'd looked at for more than a week. In L.A., gossip carried quickly—a hot ball player and his attractive director were definitely food for gossip.

"I even caught a bit in one of the trades," E. J. went on, blithely ignoring the storm clouds in Brooke's eyes. "Speculation is that Parks might take up, ah . . . show business," he said, giving her another grin, "seriously."

"Claire has a part for him if he wants it," Brooke returned, evading his obvious meaning. "It's small but meaty. I didn't want to go into it in depth with Parks until after the series. He has enough on his mind."

"Yeah, I'd say the man's had a few things on his mind for some time now."

"E. J.," Brooke began warningly as she passed over her tickets.

"You know," he continued when they fought their way through the inside crowd, "I've always wondered when somebody'd come along who'd shake that cool of yours a little."

"Is that so?" She didn't want to be amused, so she slipped her sunglasses down to conceal the humor in her eyes. "And you apparently think someone has?"

"Honey, you can't get within ten feet of the two of you and not feel the steam. I've been thinking . . ." He fussed with the front of his T-shirt as if straightening a tie. "As your close friend and associate, maybe I should ask Mr. Jones his intentions."

"Just try it, E. J., and I'll break all of your lenses." Caught between amusement and irritation, Brooke plopped down in her seat. "Sit down and buy me a hot dog."

He signaled. "What do you want on it?"

"All I can get."

"Come on, Brooke." He fished in his pocket for a couple of bills, exchanging them for hot dogs and cold drinks. "Buddy to buddy, how serious is it?"

"Not going to let up, are you?"

"I care."

Brooke glanced over at him. He was smiling, not the wisecracking grin she so often saw on his face, but a simple smile of friendship. It was, perhaps, the only weapon she had no defense against. "I'm in love with him," she said quietly. "I guess that's pretty damn serious."

"Grade-A serious," he agreed. "Congratulations."

"Am I supposed to feel like I'm walking on a cliff?" she demanded, only half-joking.

"Don't know." E. J. took a considering bite of his hot dog. "Never had the experience."

"Never been in love, E. J.?" Leaning back in her seat, Brooke grinned. "You?"

"Nope. That's why I spend so much time looking." He gave a heavy sigh. "It's a tough business, Brooke."

"Yeah." She took off his fielder's cap and swatted him with it. "I bet it is. Now shut up, they're going to announce the starting lineup."

A tough business, she thought again. Well, he wasn't far wrong, even if he had been joking. Looking for love was a lonely occupation, one she'd given up—or thought she'd given up—years before. Finding it—or having it tackle you from behind—was even tougher. Once it found you it clung, no matter how much you tried to shake it off. But she wasn't trying to shake it off, Brooke mused. She was just trying to understand how it fit and make a few adjustments. The fabric kept changing.

"Playing third and batting fourth, number twenty-nine, Parks Jones."

The already boisterous crowd went frantic as Parks jogged out on the field to take his place in the lineup. When he stood beside Snyder, he let his eyes drift over. They locked on Brooke's. With a smile, he gave the customary tip of his cap. It was a gesture for the crowd, but she knew it had been aimed at her personally. It was all the acknowledgment he would give her until it was over. It was all she expected.

"I'm going to outhit you today, Iceman," Snyder warned, grinning at the crowd. "Then Brooke's going to realize her mistake."

Parks never took his eyes off her. "She's going to marry me."

Snyder's jaw dropped. "No kidding! Well, hey . . ."

"She just doesn't know it yet," Parks added in a murmur. He slapped hands with the right fielder, batting fifth. "But she will."

Brooke detected a change in Parks's smile, something subtle, but to her unmistakable. Narrowing her eyes, she tried to decipher it. "He's up to something," she muttered.

E. J. perfected a shot with a small still camera. "What?"

"Nothing." She swirled her drink so that ice chunks banged together. "Nothing."

A well-known blues singer stepped up to the mike to sing the national anthem. Two lines of athletes removed their caps. The crowd rose, silent for what would be the last time in more than two hours. The excitement was so tangible Brooke thought she could reach out into the warm October air and grab a handful of nerves. It built and built until it exploded with cheers and shouts and whistles as the last note of the song trembled. The Kings took the field.

Sportscasters are fond of saying that the seventh game of the World Series is the ultimate in sports events—the pinnacle test of teamwork and individual effort. This was no exception. In the first inning, Brooke saw the Kings center fielder charge a ball, stretching forward to catch it on the run then holding on to it as the momentum carried him into a forward roll. She saw the Herons shortstop seem to throw heart and body after a ball to prevent it from going through the hole for a base hit. At the end of the fourth, the teams had one run apiece, each on solo home runs.

Brooke had seen Parks guard his position at third, stealing, as Lee would have put it, two certain base hits and starting the execution of a clutch double play. Watching him, Brooke realized he played this game just as he played every other—with total concentration, with steady determination. If he had nerves, if somewhere in his mind was the thought that this was *the* game, it didn't show. As he stepped up to bat, she leaned out on the rail.

Before he stepped into the box, Parks ran a hand up and down his bat as though checking for splinters. He was waiting for calm, not the calm of the shouting fans but inner calm. In his mind's eye he could see Brooke leaning on the rail, her hair tumbling over her shoulders, her eyes cool and direct. The knot of tension in his stomach eased.

When he stepped up to the plate his predominant thought was to advance the runner. With Snyder on first, he'd have to put it well out of the infield. And they'd be pitching him carefully. Both times he had come to bat, Parks had clipped a single through the hole between third and short.

Parks took his stance and looked directly into the

pitcher's eyes. He watched the windup, saw the ball hurtling toward him, shifted his weight, then checked his swing. The slider missed the corner. Ball one.

Stepping out of the box, Parks knocked the bat against his spikes to clear them of dirt. Yeah, they were going to be careful what they gave him. But he could get Snyder to second just as easily on a walk as on a hit. The trouble was, second wasn't a sure scoring position for Snyder.

The second pitch missed, low and outside. Parks checked the signal from the third base coach. He didn't allow his eyes to drift over to where Brooke sat. Parks knew even that brief contact could destroy his concentration.

The next pitch came in on him, nearly catching him on the knuckles then bouncing foul. The crowd demanded a hit. Parks checked Snyder, who was keeping very cozy with the bag, before he stepped into the box again.

Hoping to even the count, the pitcher tried another fast curve. In that fraction of a second, Parks shifted his weight. Wrists square and unbroken, he connected, letting his hips bring the bat around. He had the satisfaction of hearing the ball crack off the bat before the crowd was on its feet, screaming.

The ball sailed over center field, and though three men gave chase, no one reached it before it smashed into the dirt of the warning track and bounced high over the wall. With the fans roaring on all sides, Parks settled for the ground-rule double. There was sweat trickling down his back, but he barely felt it. He thought once that if he'd pulled the ball a bit to the right, it would have gone over clean, scoring two. Then he forgot it.

With Snyder on third, he couldn't take a sizable lead, so he contented himself with putting only a couple of feet between himself and the bag. The odds that Farlo would sacrifice to score Snyder were slim. The outfielder could spray a ball to all fields, but he wasn't a power hitter. Parks crouched, shaking his arms to keep the muscles loose.

Farlo fell behind quickly, fouling off two pitches and frustrating the crowd. Parks simply refused to think of the possibility of being stranded on base again. The infield was playing them tight, looking for that ground ball that could be turned into a double play.

Parks saw the pitch, judged it to be a low curve and tensed. Farlo showed his teeth and smacked it to right field. Parks was running on instinct before he consciously told his feet to move. The third base coach was waving him on. Years of training had Parks rounding third at top speed and heading home without hesitation or question. He saw the catcher crouched, ready to receive the ball, shielding the plate like a human wall. It flashed through Parks's mind that the Herons' right fielder was known for his arm and his precision before he threw himself at the plate in a feet-first slide that had dirt billowing in clouds. He felt the red flash of pain as his body connected with the catcher, heard his opponent's *whoosh* of air at the hit and saw the small white ball swallowed by the mitt.

They were a tangle of bodies and mutual pain as the umpire spread his arms. "Safe!"

The crowd went wild, stranger pounded on stranger, beer sloshed over cups. Brooke found that E. J. had grabbed her for a quick dance. His camera cut into her chest but it was several moments before she felt it.

"My man!" E. J. shouted, whirling her into the man on her right, who tossed his box of popcorn into the air.

No, she thought breathlessly. *My* man.

At the plate, Parks didn't concentrate on the adulation of the crowd, but on drawing enough breath into his lungs so he could stand again. The catcher's knee had slammed solidly into his ribs. Rising, he gave his uniform a perfunctory brush then headed to the dugout, where his teammates waited for him. This time, he allowed his eyes to find her. She was standing, her arms still around E. J. But her face softened with a smile that was only for him.

Touching his cap, he disappeared into the dugout. The trainer had the cold spray ready for his ribs.

Parks had forgotten his aches long before he had taken his defensive position in the top of the ninth. The Herons had whittled their lead down to one run with some blood and guts baserunning in the seventh. Since then, both teams had held like rocks. But now, Maizor was in trouble.

With only one out, he had a runner on second and a power hitter coming to the plate. We could walk him and put him on, Parks considered as the catcher tipped back his mask on his way to the mound for a conference. But the Herons had more big bats in the lineup and a few pinch hitters who couldn't be underestimated. Parks sauntered over to the mound, noting as he did that Maizor was strung tight.

"Gonna go for him?" Parks asked as the catcher chewed on a wad of gum the size of a golf ball.

"Yeah, Maizor's gonna take care of him, aren't you, Slick?"

"Sure." He turned the ball over and over in his hand. "We all want a ride in Jones's new sports car."

Parks took the mention of the Most Valuable Player

Award with a shrug. They were still two outs away, and all three men knew it. "One thing." He adjusted his cap. "Don't let him hit it toward me."

Maizor swore and grinned and visibly relaxed. "Let's play ball."

Over his shoulder, Maizor checked the runner on second. Satisfied that his lead wasn't too greedy, he fired the ball at the plate. Parks could almost hear the rush of wind as the bat cut, just over the ball. Kinjinsky called out, telling him to bear down and do it again. He did, but this time the batter got a solid piece of it.

As if a button had been pushed, Parks went for it, lunging from his side as Kinjinsky dashed to cover him. He had only seconds to judge the speed and the height. Even as he let his body fall in the direction of the ball, he felt the runner pass him on his way to third. Landing on his knees, Parks caught it on the short bounce. Without taking the time to rise, he fired the ball toward third. Kinjinsky nabbed it and held his ground as the runner slid into him.

"Still trying to make the easy plays look hard," the shortstop commented as they passed each other. They were both coated with dirt and sweat. "One more, baby, just one more."

Parks let the long, mixed roar of the crowd wash over him as he crouched at third. His face was utterly impassive. The tying run was on first. By the time the count reached three and two, being on the diamond was like being in the eye of a hurricane. Noise and turbulence whirled around them from the stands. On the field, the tension was dead silent.

Maizor went inside, handcuffing the batter. The ball was hit, drifting foul. Parks gave chase as it drifted toward the seats, running at full speed as though the wall weren't looming up in front of him. He could get it, he knew he could get it—if an excited fan didn't reach over and make a grab.

With his free hand, he caught the rail and lifted his glove. He felt the impact of the ball as he closed the leather over it. While the crowd started to scream, he found he was looking directly into Brooke's eyes. The foul had all but fallen into her lap.

"Nice catch." Leaning over, she kissed him full on the mouth.

Then one of his teammates had him around the waist, and the rest was madness.

Parks had more champagne dumped on him than he could possibly have drunk. It mixed with sweat and washed some of the grime away. Snyder had positioned himself on top of a locker and from there emptied two bottles on anyone in sight—reporters and league brass included. Accused of showboating, Parks was tossed, fully dressed, into the whirlpool. Grateful, he stripped and remained where he was with half a bottle of champagne. From there he gave interviews while the water beat the aches from his body and bedlam raged around him.

The pitch on his double had been an outside fast ball. Yeah, his slide into home had been risky, considering the arm of the right fielder, but he'd had a good lead. He continued to answer questions as Snyder, in a champagne-drenched uniform, was not so gently assisted into the whirlpool with him. Parks slid down farther in the soothing water and drained the cold wine straight from the bottle. Yes, the redhead in the stands was Brooke Gordon, his director on the de Marco commercials. Parks smiled as Snyder wisecracked the reporters' attention to himself. Teammates might poke and prod into each other's business, but they protected their own.

Parks closed his eyes a moment, just a moment. He wanted to recapture that instant when she had leaned over and touched her lips to his. Everything had been heightened in that split second of victory. He had thought he could hear each individual shout from the crowd. He'd seen the sunlight glint on the chipped paint of the railing, felt the baking heat as his hand had wrapped around it. Then he'd seen her eyes, close, soft, beautiful. Her voice had been quiet, conveying excitement, humor and love all in two words. When they had touched his, her lips had been warm and smooth, and for an instant that had been all he had felt. Just the silky texture of her lips. He hadn't even heard the last out called. When he'd been dragged back on the field by his teammates, she had simply lowered her chin to the rail and smiled at him. *Later*. He had heard her thought as clearly as if she had spoken it.

It took two hours to urge the last reporter out of the clubhouse. The players were quieting. The first rush of victory was over, replaced by a mellowness that would very quickly become nostalgia. The year was over. There'd be no more infield practice, batting practice, night rides on planes with card games and snoring. They were in a business where today was over quickly and tomorrow took all their efforts. Now there wasn't a tomorrow, but next year.

Some were sitting, talking quietly on the benches in

the midst of the locker room litter, as Parks dressed. He glanced at the second-string catcher, a boy of barely nineteen, completing his first year in the majors. He held his shin guards in his hands as if he couldn't bear to part with them. Parks put his mitt into his duffel bag and felt suddenly old.

"How're the ribs?" Kinjinsky asked as he slung his own bag over his shoulder.

"Fine." Parks gestured to the boy on the bench. "The kid's barely old enough to vote."

"Yeah." Kinjinsky, a ripe thirty-two, grinned. "It's hell, isn't it?" They both laughed as Parks closed his locker for the last time that year. "See you in the spring, Jones. My woman's waiting for me."

Parks zipped up his bag while the thought warmed in him. He, too, had a woman, and it would take him thirty minutes to drive to the mountains.

"Hey, Parks." Snyder caught him before he'd reached the door. "You really going to marry her?"

"As soon as I can talk her into it."

Snyder nodded, not questioning the phrasing of the answer. "Give me a call when you set it up. I'm the best man."

With a smile, Parks held out a hand and shook the beefy one. "Damned if you're not, George." He walked into the corridor, closing the door on the clubhouse and the season.

When he emerged outside, it was dusk. Only a few fans lingered, but he signed autographs for them and gave them the time they wanted. Parks thought idly about picking up another bottle of champagne for himself and Brooke as he signed his name to the bill of a twelve-year-old's battered hat. Champagne, a fire burning low, candles. It seemed like a good setting to propose marriage. It was going to be tonight, because tonight he didn't think he could lose.

The parking lot was all but deserted. The overhead lights were just flickering on as twilight deepened. Then he saw her. Brooke was sitting on the hood of his car, spotlighted in the flood of a security light, her hair like tongues of flame around her strong-boned, delicate-skinned face. Love welled up in him, a fierce possessive love that took his breath away. Except for the lips that curved, she didn't move. He realized then she had been watching him for some time. He struggled to regain some control over his muscles before he continued toward her.

"If I'd known you were waiting here, I'd have come out sooner." He felt the ache in his ribs again, but not from the bruise this time. This was from a need he was still not quite used to.

"I told E. J. to take my car. I didn't mind waiting." Reaching up, she put both hands on his shoulders. "Congratulations."

Very deliberately, Parks set his bag down on the asphalt then dove his hands into her hair. Their eyes held briefly, endlessly, before he lowered his mouth and took what he needed.

His emotions were more finely tuned than he had realized. All the pleasure of victory, the weariness that came from winning it, the dregs of excitement and tension surfaced, to be doubled then swept away by one all-encompassing need. Brooke. How was he to have known that she would grow to be everything—and all things? A bit unnerved by the intensity, Parks drew away. A man couldn't win when his knees were buckling. He ran his knuckles down her cheek, wanting to see that very faint, very arousing clouding of her eyes.

"I love you."

At his words, Brooke rested her head against his chest and breathed deeply. She could smell his shower on him, some subtle soap fragrance that spoke of gymnasiums and locker rooms that were inhabited only by men. For some reason, it made her feel acutely a woman. The light grew dimmer as they remained, held close and silent.

"Too tired to celebrate?" she murmured.

"Uh-uh." He kissed her hair.

"Good." Drawing away, she slid from the hood. "I'll buy you dinner to start it off." Brooke opened the passenger door and smiled. "Hungry?"

Until that moment, Parks hadn't realized that he was starving. What little he'd eaten before the game had been devoured by nerves. "Yeah. Do I get to pick the place?"

"Sky's the limit."

Fifteen minutes later, Brooke gazed around the garishly colored Hamburger Heaven. "You know," she mused, studying the overhead lights that were shaped like sesame seed rolls, "I'd forgotten your penchant for junk food."

"A hundred percent pure beef," Parks claimed, picking up an enormous double-decker sandwich.

"If you believe that, you believe anything."

Grinning, he offered her a French fry. "Cynic."

"If you call me names, I won't read you the sports page." She put her hand over the folded paper she'd just bought. "Then you won't hear the accolades the press have heaped on you." When he shrugged, unconcerned, she opened the paper. "Well, I want to hear them." With one hand on her milkshake, Brooke began to thumb her way through. "Here . . . Oh." She stopped dead and scowled.

"What is it?" Parks leaned over. On the front page were two pictures, side by side. The first was of his over-the-seats catch of the final out. The second was of Brooke's impulsive kiss. The caption read:

JONES SCORES . . . TWICE

"Cute," he decided, "considering I didn't score but snagged a pop fly." He twisted his head, skimming down the article which ran through the highlights of the game—critiques and praise. "Hmm. . . . 'And Jones ended it with a race to the rail, snagging Hennesey's long foul out of the seats in one of the finest plays of the afternoon. As usual, the MVP makes the impossible look routine. He got his reward from the luscious redhead'—here he shot Brooke a brief glance—'Brooke Gordon, a successful commercial director who's been seen with the third baseman on and off the set.' "

"I really hate that," Brooke said with such vehemence that Parks looked up in surprise.

"Hate what?"

"Having my picture splashed around that way. And this—this half-baked speculation. This, and that silly business in the *Times* a couple days ago."

"The one that called you a willowy, titian-haired gypsy with smoky eyes?"

"It's not funny, Parks." Brooke shoved the paper aside.

"It's not tragic, either," he pointed out.

"They should mind their own business."

Leaning back, Parks nibbled on a fry. "You'd probably be the first to tell me that being in the public eye
makes you public property."

Brooke scowled at that, knowing they were precisely
her words when they'd discussed the poster deal.
"*You're* in the public eye," she countered. "It's the way
you make your living. *I* don't. I work behind the camera,
and I have a right to my privacy."

"Ever heard of guilty by association?" He smiled
before she could retort. Instead of a curt remark, she let
out a long sigh. "At least they're accurate," he added.
"I've often thought of you as a gypsy myself."

Brooke picked up her cheeseburger, frowned, then bit
into it. "I still don't like it," she muttered. "I
think . . ." She shrugged, not certain how foolish she
was going to sound. "I've always been a little overly
sensitive about my privacy, and now . . . what's happening between us is too important for me to want to
share with anyone who has fifty cents for a paper."

Parks leaned forward again and took her hand.
"That's nice," he said softly. "That's very nice."

The tone of his voice had fresh emotion rising in her.
"I don't want to hole up like a couple of hermits, Parks,
but I don't want every move we make to be on the
evening news, either."

With a bit more nonchalance than he was feeling at the
moment, he shrugged and began to eat again. "Romance
is news. . . . So's divorce, when it involves public
people."

"It's not going to ease up with the de Marco campaign, either, or if you decide to take that part in the

film.'' She took another French fry out of its paper scoop and glared at it. ''The hotter you are, the more the press will buzz around. It's maddening.''

''I could break my contract,'' he suggested.

''Don't be ridiculous.''

''There's another solution,'' he considered, watching Brooke swallow the French fry and reach for another.

''What?''

''We could get married. Want some salt for those?''

Brooke stared at him, then found she had to search for her voice. ''What did you say?''

''I asked if you wanted some salt.'' Parks offered her a tiny paper packet. ''No?'' he said when she neither answered nor moved. ''I also said we could get married.''

''Married?'' Brooke echoed stupidly. ''You and me?''

''The press would ease off after a while. Quietly married couples don't make news the same way lovers do. Human nature.'' He pushed his sandwich aside and leaned toward her. ''What do you think?''

''I think you're crazy,'' Brooke managed in a whisper. ''And I don't think this is funny.''

Parks gripped her arm when she started to scoot out of the booth. ''I'm not joking.''

''You—you want to get married so we won't get our picture in the paper?''

''I don't give a damn if we get our picture in the paper or not, you do.''

''So you want to get married to—to placate me.'' She stopped struggling against his hold on her arm, but her eyes filled with fury.

''I've never had any intention of placating you,'' he

countered. "I couldn't placate you if I dedicated my life to it. I want to get married because I'm in love with you. I'm *going* to marry you," he corrected, suddenly angry, "if I have to drag you, kicking and screaming."

"Is that so?"

"Yes, that's exactly so. You might as well get used to it."

"Maybe I don't want to get married." Brooke shoved the food in front of them aside. "What about that?"

"Too bad." He leaned back, eyeing her with the same simmering temper with which she eyed him. *"I* want to get married."

"And that's supposed to be enough, huh?"

"It's enough for me."

Brooke crossed her arms over her chest and glared at him. "Kicking and screaming?"

"If that's the way you want it."

"I can bite, too."

"So can I."

Her heart was thudding against her ribs, but Brooke realized it wasn't from anger. No, it had nothing to do with anger. He was sitting there, across a laminated table littered with food from a twelve-year-old's fantasy, telling her he was going to marry her whether she liked it or not. Brooke discovered, somewhat to her own amazement, that she liked it just fine. But she wasn't going to make it easy for him.

"Maybe winning the series went to your head, Parks. It's going to take more than a temper tantrum to get me to marry you."

"What do you want?" he demanded. "Candlelight and soft music?" Annoyed that he had scuttled his own plans, he leaned over again and grabbed her hands.

"You're not the kind of woman who needs scenery, Brooke; you know just how easy it is to come by and how little it means. What the hell do you want?"

"Take two," she said very calmly. "You know your motivation," she began in her cool director's voice, "but this time tone down the force and try for a little finesse. Ask," she suggested, looking into his eyes, "don't tell."

He felt the anger, or perhaps it had been fear, slide out of him. The hands that held hers gentled. "Brooke"—he lifted a hand and pressed her fingers to his lips—"will you marry me?" Parks smiled over their joined hands. "How was that?"

Brooke laced the fingers with hers. "Perfect."

Chapter 11

WHAT WAS SHE DOING? IN A SUDDEN PANIC, BROOKE stared at herself in the free standing full-length mirror. How could things be happening so fast and be so much out of her control? A year ago—no, even six months ago—she hadn't known Parks Jones existed. In something under an hour, she would be married to him. Committed. For life. Forever.

From somewhere deep inside her brain came a panicked call to run and run fast. Brooke hadn't realized she'd made a move until she was summarily jerked back into place.

"Be still, Ms. Gordon," Billings ordered firmly. "There are two dozen of these little buttons if there's one." She used a complaining tone, though privately she thought Brooke's choice of an ivory satin gown with its snug bodice and flowing skirt was inspired. A good, traditional wedding dress, she decided, not one of those

flighty trouser suits or miniskirted affairs in scarlet or
fuchsia. Billings continued to fasten the range of tiny
pearl buttons in back.

"Stand still now," she ordered again as Brooke
fidgeted.

"Billings," Brooke said weakly, "I really think I'm
going to be sick."

The housekeeper looked up at Brooke's reflection.
Her face was pale, her eyes huge, made darker by the
merest touch of slate-gray shadow. In Billings's staunch
opinion, a bride was supposed to look ready to faint.
"Nonsense," she said briskly. "Just a case of the
flutters."

"Flutters," Brooke repeated, creasing her brow. "I
never flutter. That's ridiculous."

The Englishwoman smiled fleetingly as Brooke
straightened her shoulders. "Flutters, jitters, nerves—
every woman born has them on her wedding day."

"Well, I don't," she claimed as her stomach muscles
quivered.

Billings only sniffed as she finished her fastening.
"There now, that's the last one."

"Thank God," Brooke muttered, heading for a chair
before Billings caught her.

"No, you don't. You're not putting creases in that
skirt."

"Billings, for heaven's sake—"

"A woman has to suffer now and again."

Brooke's opinion was a short four-letter word. Lifting
a brow, Billings picked up a hairbrush from the vanity.
"A fine way for a blushing bride to talk."

"I'm not a blushing bride." Brooke swept away
before Billings could apply the brush. "I'm twenty-eight

years old," she continued, pacing. "I must be crazy, I must be absolutely crazy. No sane woman agrees to marry a man in a fast-food restaurant."

"You're getting married in Ms. Thorton's garden," Billings corrected. "And it's quite a lovely day for it."

The practical tone caused Brooke to scowl. "And I should never have let her talk me into that, either."

"Hah!" The exclamation had Brooke's brows lifting. Billings gestured threateningly with the hairbrush. "Hah!" she said again, effectively closing Brooke's mouth. "No one talks you into anything. You're a hard-headed, stubborn, single-minded young woman, and you're shaking in your shoes because there's a hard-headed, stubborn, single-minded young man downstairs who's going to give you a run for your money."

"I certainly am not shaking in my shoes," Brooke corrected, insulted. Billings saw the faint pink flush rise to the pale cheeks.

"Scared to death."

Brooke stuck both fists on her hips. "I am most certainly not afraid of Parks Jones."

"Hah!" Billings repeated as she pulled over a footstool. Climbing on it, she began to draw the brush through Brooke's hair. "You'll probably stammer and quake when you take your vows, just like some silly girl who doesn't know her own mind."

"I've never stammered in my life." Enunciating each word precisely, Brooke glared at their twin reflections in the mirror. "And nothing makes me quake."

"We'll just see about that, won't we?" Rather pleased with herself, Billings arranged Brooke's mane of hair into a cunningly tumbled mass. In this, she secured a delicate clip of pale-pink-and-white hibiscus. She had fussed that lily of the valley or rosebuds would have been more suitable, but secretly thought the exotic flowers were stunning.

"Now, where are those lovely pearl drops Ms. Thorton gave you?"

"Over there." Still fuming, Brooke pointed to the tiny jeweler's box that held Claire's gift.

They should have eloped as Parks had suggested, Brooke thought. What had made her think she wanted all this fuss and bother? What had made her think she wanted to get married in the first place? As her nerves started jumping again, she caught Billings's ironic stare. Brooke lifted her chin.

"Well, put them on," the housekeeper ordered, holding the pink-blushed pearls in her palm. "It was very clever of Mr. Jones to send you flowers to match them."

"If you like him so much, why don't you marry him?" Brooke muttered, fastening the earrings with fingers that refused to stop trembling.

"I suppose you'll do," Billings said briskly, swallowing a lump in her throat. "Even without a proper veil and train." She wanted badly to press a kiss to Brooke's cheek, but knew it would weaken both of them. "Come along, then," she said instead. "It's time."

I could still call it off, Brooke thought as she let Billings draw her down the hall. There's still time. No one can make me go through with this. The little skips of nerves in her stomach had increased to thumps. There's absolutely nothing that can make me walk out into that garden. What was the phrase? she wondered. Marry in haste, repent at leisure? This was certainly haste.

It had only been four days since Parks had asked her. Four days. Maybe the big mistake had been in telling

Claire. Good God, she'd never seen anyone move so fast once they'd gotten the bit between their teeth. Brooke decided she must have been in a state of shock to have let Claire sweep her along with plans and arrangements. An intimate ceremony in her terraced garden, a champagne reception. *Elope?* Claire had brushed that aside with a wave of her hand. Elopements were for silly teenagers. And wouldn't a three-piece ensemble be lovely? Brooke had found herself caught up. And now she was just caught.

But no, Brooke corrected as she and Billings reached the foot of the stairs. All she had to do was turn around and head for the door. She could get into her car and just drive away. That was the coward's way. Straightening her shoulders, Brooke rejected it. She wouldn't run, she would simply walk outside and explain very calmly that she had changed her mind. Yes, that's all it would take. I'm very sorry, she practiced mentally, but I've decided not to get married after all. She'd be very calm and very firm.

"Oh, Brooke, you look lovely." And there was Claire, dressed in powder-blue silk with the sheen of tears in her eyes.

"Claire, I—"

"Absolutely lovely. I wish you'd let me have them play the wedding march."

"No, I—"

"It doesn't matter, as long as you're happy." Claire pressed her cheek to Brooke's. "Isn't it silly, I feel just like a mother. Imagine having your first pangs of motherhood at my age."

"Oh, Claire."

"No, no, I'm not going to get sloppy and sentimental

and ruin my face." Sniffling, she drew away. "It's not every day I'm maid of honor."

"Claire, I want to—"

"They're waiting, Ms. Thorton."

"Yes, yes, of course." Giving Brooke's hand a quick squeeze, she went out on the terrace.

"Now you, Ms. Gordon." Brooke stood where she was, wondering if the coward's way wasn't basically sound. Billings put a firm hand on her back and pushed. Brooke found herself out on the terrace facing Parks.

He took her hand. His was firm as he brought hers to his lips. She noticed his eyes, smiling, sure. He was in a pearl-gray suit, more formal than anything she had seen him wear. But his eyes held that complete intensity she knew they had when he waited for a pitch. She found herself walking with him to the center of the terrace that was surrounded by flowers and the ornamental trees Claire loved.

Still time, Brooke thought as the minister began to speak in a calm, clear voice. But she couldn't open her mouth to stop what was already happening.

She'd remember the scent always. Jasmine and vanilla, and the sweet drift of baby roses. But she didn't see the flowers because her eyes were locked on Parks's. He was repeating the words the minister spoke, the traditional words spoken countless times by countless couples. But she heard them as if they were uttered for the first time.

Love, honor, cherish.

She felt the ring slip onto her finger. Felt, but again didn't see because she couldn't take her eyes from his. From the branches of a weeping cherry, a bird began to trill.

She heard her own voice, strong and assured, repeat the same promises. And her hand, with no trembling, placed the symbol of the promise on Parks's finger.

A pledge, a promise, a gift. Then their lips moved together, sealing it.

I was going to run, she remembered.

"I'd have caught you," Parks murmured against her mouth.

Astonished and annoyed, Brooke drew back. He was grinning at her, his hands still caught in her hair. To the confusion of the others in the quiet, fragrant garden, Brooke cursed him then threw her arms around his neck and laughed.

"Hey." Snyder gave Parks a firm shove. "Give somebody else a chance."

Claire's idea of a small gathering was the epitome of a producer's understatement. Though Brooke didn't bother to count heads, she knew there were well over a hundred "absolutely essential guests." She found she didn't mind—the glitter was her gift to Claire. There was a bubbly fountain of champagne, a five-tiered pink-and-white cake and silver platters of food that for once Brooke had no interest in. Which turned out for the best, as she was swept from one person's arms to another, kissed, hugged and congratulated until it all became a blur of color and sound.

She met Parks's mother, a tiny, exquisite woman who kissed her cheek then burst into tears. His father crushed Brooke in a hug and murmured that now that Parks was married, he would stop the nonsense and come into the company. She found herself inheriting a family in a lump—a large, confusing family that didn't quite fit any of the imaginings of her youth. And through it all, she had barely more than glimpses of Parks as she was passed from cousin to cousin to be weighed, measured and discussed like a fascinating new acquisition.

"Leave the girl be a minute." A sturdy, pewter-haired woman swept the others aside with an imperious wave of her hand. "These Joneses are a silly bunch." She sighed, then summed Brooke up with one long look. "I'm your Aunt Lorraine," she said and extended her hand.

Brooke accepted the handshake, knowing instinctively the gesture was somehow more sincere and more intimate than all the kisses she had received. Then with a flash of insight, she knew. "The gold piece."

Lorraine smiled, pleased. "Told you about that, did he? Well, he's a good boy . . . more or less." A straight, no-nonsense brow lifted. "And he won't bully you, will he?"

With a grin, Brooke shook her head. "No, ma'am, he won't."

Lorraine nodded, giving Brooke's hand a quick pat. "Good. I'll expect a visit in six months. It takes a couple that long to work out the first kinks. Now, if I were you, I'd get my husband and sneak out of this rabble." With this advice, she strode away. Brooke had her first twinge of genuine kinship.

Even so, it seemed like hours before they could slip away. Brooke had intended to steal back upstairs and change, but Parks had seen his opportunity and had pulled her outside, bundled her into his car and driven off. Now he stopped the car in the driveway of the A-frame and sighed.

"We made it."

"It was rude," Brooke mused.

"Yeah."

"And very smart." Leaning over, she kissed him. "Especially since you managed to cop a bottle of champagne on the way."

"Quick hands," he explained as he stepped from the car.

Brooke chuckled, but felt a fresh ripple of unease as they walked up the path. Parks's hand was closed over hers. She could feel the slight, unfamiliar pressure of her wedding ring against her skin. "One problem," she began, pushing the feeling aside. "You dragged me out of there without my purse." She glanced at the door, then back at Parks. "No keys."

Parks reached in his pocket and drew out his own. A faint frown creased her brow as she remembered he had a key to the door now. A key to her life. Though he noticed her reaction, Parks said nothing, only slipping the key into the lock. It opened silently. He swept her up into his arms, and with her laughter, the subtle disharmony was forgotten.

"I hadn't realized you were such a traditionalist," Brooke murmured, nuzzling at his neck, "but . . ." She trailed off at the sound of high, sharp yapping. Astonished, she looked down to see a small brown dog with a black muzzle racing around Parks's feet, making occasional dives for his ankles. "What's that?" she managed.

"Your wedding present." With his toe, he nudged the puppy, sending him rolling over on his back. "Homely enough?"

Brooke stared down at the pushed-in mongrel face.

"Oh, Parks," she whispered, close to tears. "You fool."

"E. J. should've dropped him off about an hour ago, if he was on schedule. Guy at the pound thought I was crazy when I told him I wanted something down-to-the-ground homely."

"Oh, I love you!" Brooke squeezed his neck fiercely then wriggled out of his arms. In her satin wedding dress, she knelt on the floor to play with the puppy.

She looked young, Parks thought, too young, as she buried her face in the little dog's fur. Why would he constantly expose her vulnerabilities then be uncertain how to handle them? There was so much sweetness in her, and yet, was he somehow more comfortable with the vinegar she could serve him? It was the mix, Parks thought as he knelt to join her, the fascinating mix he couldn't resist.

"Our first child." Brooke chuckled when the puppy lay in exhausted slumber on the rug.

"He has your nose."

"And your feet," she retorted. "He's going to be enormous from the size of them."

"Maybe you can cast him in a few dog food commercials," he commented as he drew Brooke to her feet. Gently he kissed her cheek, then trailed his lips over her chin to the other one. He felt the sudden tremble of her breath on his skin. "Champagne's getting warm," he murmured.

"I'm not thirsty."

He was leading her slowly toward the stairs, still planting those soft, whispering kisses over her face on the journey, leaving her lips—her heating, seeking lips—subtly tormented. And they started to climb the stairs, without rush or hurry, while Parks began unfastening that long range of tiny buttons.

"How many are there?" he murmured against her mouth.

"Dozens," Brooke answered, loosening his tie as they reached the halfway point.

His fingers were nimble. Before they reached the door of the bedroom, he had the gown loosened to her waist. Brooke pushed the jacket from his shoulder, and with her teeth nipping at his neck, tugged his shirt from the waistband of his pants.

"Are you ever going to kiss me?" she demanded breathlessly.

"Mm-hmm." But he only drove her mad by running his lips over her shoulder as he nudged the satin aside. Then he drew it from her, running his hands slowly down her body until the material was only a pool of white at her feet. He toyed with the bits of lace she wore, tiny, filmy wisps designed to torment men. And even as they tormented him, Parks fought for control. There was always that last struggle for control before he found he was lost in her.

Her fingers slid down his naked ribs to brush over his stomach before she found the hook to his trousers. She heard his quick, indrawn breath before his hands became more demanding. Needing, wanting, she pulled him with her onto the bed.

Why should there be such desperation when they were now so securely bound to each other? Though neither of them understood it, they both felt it. The urgency to touch, taste. To possess. Gentleness was abandoned while hungry, primitive passion took its place. The teasing kisses stopped with a hard, burning pressure of mouth on mouth. Her hands sought, as skillfully as his, to find weaknesses. Every moan brought a fresh thrill of arousal, each sigh an increase of tortuous desire until neither knew if the sounds were from pleasure or desperation. And both refused to succumb to the fire.

He found her breast taut and firm. Greedily, his mouth sought it, sending a tearing thread of delight into the core of her. Even as she moaned in surrender, her hands pressed him closer, her body moving sinuously under his until he was lost in the taste of her.

Flesh heated against flesh. The pace quickened. Faster, faster until they were breathless and clinging but still not ready to yield. She ran her hands over his damp back, over the roping of muscles that accented his superior strength. But physical strength meant nothing in the inescapable quicksand of passion. They were both trapped in it, both equally incapable of freeing themselves.

With sudden strength, she shifted, so that they were tangled together, side by side. Her mouth fastened on his, devouring as eagerly as she was devoured, taking as mindlessly as she was taken. Her hair fell over them, curtaining their faces so that Parks couldn't breathe without breathing her. If he had been capable of thought, he might have imagined himself absorbed by her. But there was no thought for either of them, and the need had grown too great to be resisted.

She went willingly when he shifted her, drawing his mouth down to hers even as he entered her with something close to violence. Then there was only speed and heat, driving them beyond everything but each other.

"Should I need you more each time?" Brooke wondered aloud.

"Mmm." Parks didn't want to move from the warm comfort of her body. It yielded under his, pressed deep into the mattress. "Just don't stop."

It was dusk. The light filtering through the windows was soft—and soon it would be night. Her wedding night. Yet she still felt only like a lover. How would it be to feel like a wife? Lifting her hand, she stared at the band on her finger. It was encrusted with diamonds and sapphires that glowed softly in the room's twilight. "I don't want it to be different tomorrow," she thought aloud. "I don't want it to change."

Parks raised his head. "Everything changes. You'll get mad if I use all the hot water for my shower. I'll get mad if you've drunk the last of the coffee."

Brooke laughed. "You have a way of simplifying things."

"Those are the nuts and bolts of a relationship, Mrs. Jones," he claimed and kissed her.

The eyes that had begun to close for the kiss opened wide. "Jones," she repeated. "I'd forgotten about that part of it." She considered for a minute. "It makes me think of your mother . . . though of course I thought she was very nice."

Parks gave a muffled chuckle. "Don't worry. Just remember she lives three hundred miles away."

Brooke rolled over until she lay on top of him. "You have a very nice family."

"Yeah, and we don't want to get tangled up with them any more than we have to."

"Well . . ." Brooke laid her head on his chest. "No. At least not too soon," she added, thinking of his aunt. She relaxed again as he began to lazily stroke her hair. "Parks?"

"Hmm?"

"I'm glad we decided to come here instead of flying off somewhere."

"We'll go to Maui for a couple of weeks around Christmas. I want you to see my place there."

Brooke thought of her schedule if she decided to take Claire up on the feature for cable. Somehow or other, she'd manage to get the two weeks. "I love you."

His hand stopped a moment, then pressed her closer. They were three words she didn't say often. "Did I tell you how beautiful you looked when Billings shoved you out on the terrace?"

Brooke's head shot up. "You saw that?"

Grinning, he traced her ear with his fingertip. "Funny, I didn't expect you to be as terrified as I was."

Brooke regarded him a moment, then a smile curved on her lips. "Were you really?"

"A half hour before the wedding, I'd run up a list of all the reasons why we should call it off."

She lifted a brow. "Were there many?"

"I lost count," he told her, ignoring the narrowing of her eyes. "I could only think of one good reason to go through with it."

"Oh, really?" Her chin came up as she tossed her head. "And what was that?"

"I love you."

Brooke dropped her forehead onto his. "That's it, huh?"

"The only one I could think of." He slid a hand down to her hip. "Though one or two others are beginning to occur to me."

"Mmm. Like it being good for the campaign." She began to nuzzle, just behind his ear.

"Oh, sure. That's top on my list." He groaned when the first shudder rippled through him. "Right next to having somebody to sort my socks."

"You can forget that one," Brooke murmured, moving down to his shoulder. "But there's always having an in with the director when you do that part for cable."

"Haven't decided to do it." His legs tangled with hers as they altered positions. "Have you?"

"Not yet." Her thoughts began to drift as he cupped her breast. "But you should."

"Why?"

Lazily, her eyes opened to look into his. "I shouldn't tell you."

Intrigued, he propped himself on his elbow and toyed with her hair. "Why not?"

She sighed a little, while managing to convey a shrug. "The last thing you need is someone feeding your ego."

"Go ahead." He kissed her nose. "I can take it."

"Damn it, Parks, you're good."

He stopped in the action of twining her hair around his finger and stared at her. "What did you say?"

Brooke shifted again. "Well, I don't mean you can *act*," she began. "Don't start getting delusions."

He grinned, enjoying her ironic lift of brow. "That's more like it."

"You have good camera presence," she went on.

"Do you have any idea how many big stars stay big simply by playing themselves?" Parks grunted, more interested in the taste at the curve of her shoulder. "You know how to play yourself, Parks," Brooke persisted, drawing him back for a moment. "And if you were to stick to parts, at least for a while, that suited you . . . well, when you really are ready to retire from baseball you could walk right into a movie career."

He started to laugh, then stopped when he saw the look in her eyes. "You're not joking."

Brooke stared at him, then let out a long breath. "I'm really going to hate myself when I've got to deal with you as a director in a couple of weeks, but you're very, very good, and you should think about it. And if you get a star complex when I tell you to run through some business on camera a half a dozen times, I'll . . ."

"What?" he challenged.

"Something," Brooke said ominously. "Something despicable."

He gave her a wicked grin. "Promise?"

Since she couldn't stop the laugh, she rolled him over forcibly so that she was lying across him again. "Yeah. And now I'm going to make love with you until your bones dissolve."

"Is this in my contract?" he demanded.

"You better believe it."

Chapter 12

THOUGH IT WAS NOVEMBER, LOS ANGELES WAS SUF-
fering from a heat wave that fried tempers and melted
patience. Brooke's was no exception. She and Parks had
had ten long, isolated days before she had begun work
again—but they hadn't been trouble-free. Nothing's
trouble-free, Brooke reminded herself as she knotted her
blouse beneath her breasts. What fool thought a honey-
moon would be? She had, she admitted ruefully as the
camera crane was unloaded. But then how much thought
had she really given to adjustments, to changes and, as
Parks had termed it, the nuts and bolts business that
made up a marriage?

She had accepted his name, and though she would
keep her own professionally, it was Brooke Jones that
she would sign to all legal documents. He had given up
his apartment and moved into her house. She had his

name, he had her key. Why did she feel she was tallying a balance sheet? Frustrated, Brooke wiped her forearm over her brow.

Was that what marriage was, she wondered, a series of checks and balances? With her marriage barely three weeks old, she should be blissfully happy, glowing. Instead, Brooke felt frustrated, annoyed and unsettled— perhaps more unsettled because she knew Parks was no more blissfully happy than she.

With a shake of her head, she told herself to put it aside. Bringing her personal problems to work wouldn't solve them—and more than likely it would make them worse, since she was directing Parks.

"Let's go up, E. J., I want to see the angle." Sitting in the basket beside him, she gave the crane operator a nod to take them up.

Below them, the beach spread gold. The surf kicked up, white and frothy, catching the glint of the sun and rainbowing through the lens. She thought she could feel the heat steam from the metal casing of the camera. "All right, I'll want a wide shot when he starts, then zoom in, but not too tight. At this angle, we'll get a good profile of the horse. The palomino's a nice contrast with the jeans. Set the speed. I want it slow enough so they see every muscle ripple."

"On Parks or the horse?" E. J. asked with a grin.

"On both," Brooke answered curtly, nodding to be brought down. Wiping her palms on the seat of her pants, she strode over to where Parks waited. He wore nothing but snug, low-slung de Marco jeans. "We're ready for you."

"All right." Parks gave her a long, steady look as he

hooked his thumbs in his front pockets. He wasn't sure why he was dissatisfied, or why he felt the need to annoy her. The friction had been growing between them for the past few days, building and shifting like some electric storm. But there'd been no boom of thunder, no slash of lightning to release the pressure. "What do you want?"

"You've seen the script," she reminded him.

"Aren't you going to give me my motivation?"

"Don't be a smart aleck, Parks," she snapped. "It's too damn hot."

"Just want to make sure I've got the right mood so you won't make me do it a half dozen times."

Temper flared in her eyes and was forcefully suppressed. She wouldn't let him taunt her into a public sniping. "You'll do it two dozen times if I feel it's necessary," she said as calmly as possible. "Now get on the horse, gallop straight down the beach in the shallows. And enjoy it."

"Is that an order?" he murmured, deceptively mild.

"It's a direction," she returned evenly. "I'm the director, you're the talent. Got it?"

"Yeah, I got it." Catching her close, he crushed her mouth with his. He felt the dampness of her blouse under his palm, the angry rigidity of her body and the yielding softness of her breasts. Why was he angry? he wondered even as his temper inched higher. Why did he feel he was dragging her close and shoving her away at the same time? "Got that?" he demanded as he turned and swung onto the horse.

She glared at him, a half-naked man astride a golden horse, as he smiled down at her with the cocky assurance she both loved and detested. Making him pay for that small victory would be a pleasure. Turning on her heel, Brooke strode back to her crew. "Take one," she ordered, then waited, turning ideas for vengeance over in her mind. She took the bullhorn her assistant handed her. "Places!" Parks led the palomino into the surf. Brooke stared at him, forcing herself to put her personal feelings on hold while she thought and felt and saw only as a director. "Roll film, and . . . action!"

He's magnificent, Brooke thought with a twin surge of pride and irritation. He took the horse into an easy, rolling gallop, kicking up the surf so that the streams of water rose high. Beads glistened on his skin, darkly tanned so that he and the palomino merged into one golden form. Parks's hair and the horse's mane lifted in the wind the motion caused. Strength, an elegance of movement and the simplicity of two beautiful animals. Brooke didn't need special effects to show her how it would look in slow motion.

"Cut. E. J.?"

"Fantastic," he called down. "Sales of de Marco jeans just went up ten percent."

"Let's make sure." Pulling her damp shirt away from her back, Brooke walked to where Parks waited, astride the horse. It had been fantastic, she mused, but not perfect. Spotting her, Parks broke off his conversation with the palomino's trainer.

"Well?"

"It looked pretty good. Let's do it again."

"Why?"

Ignoring the question, she absently patted the gelding's smooth throat. "I want you to look down the beach as you ride . . . all the way down." She didn't want that comfortable, free-wheeling sexuality this time, but a dash of aloofness, the solitary-man appeal flavored with the sensuality any female over twelve would recognize.

He shifted in the saddle, his eyes never leaving hers. "Why?"

"Ride the horse, Parks," she countered. "Let me sell the jeans."

Very slowly, he dismounted. The trainer quickly remembered something he had to do somewhere else. Behind them, the crew became very busy. Parks held the reins in one hand while he and Brooke measured each other. "Ever considered asking?" he said quietly.

"Ever considered following directions?" she tossed back.

He felt the salt spray drying on his skin. "Too bad you've never been a team player, Brooke."

"This isn't a ball game," she retorted, firing up. "We all have our jobs to do. Yours is whatever I tell you it is."

The flash of anger in his eyes suited her mood. She wanted a fight, a rip-roaring screamer that would tear through the tension of their last few days together. Planting her feet, Brooke prepared to attack and defend.

"No," he said with a sudden deadly calm that put her at a disadvantage, "it's not. My job is to endorse de Marco."

"And that's what I'm telling you to do." She forced herself to match his tone, though she badly wanted to shout. "If you want to be a prima donna, wait until after we wrap. Take your complaints and talk to your agent."

His hand snaked out to grab her arm before she could stalk away. "I'm talking to my wife."

Heart hammering in her throat, she looked down at the

hand that held her. "Your director," Brooke icily
corrected, meeting his eyes. "My crew's hot, Parks. I'd
like to finish this before someone faints from heat
exhaustion."

His grip tightened. But he saw that her face was
flushed from the heat and damp with sweat. "We're not
finished with this," he told her as he released her arm.
"This time, you're going to take a good hard look at the
rules." Swinging onto the horse, Parks rode away before
she could think of an appropriate comment.

Brooke frowned after him as she stalked back to the
crane. "Take two."

He could have given no logical, succinct explanation
for his anger. Parks only knew he was furious. He had
only one motivation as he stalked down the corridors to
Brooke's office—to have it out with her. He wasn't
certain what *it* was, but he would have had it out with her
on location if she hadn't been gone before he'd realized
it. Though he wasn't thrilled about coming to terms with
her in her office, he'd had plenty of experience in
meeting a challenge on the opposition's home field. All
it meant was that he would take the offensive first.

Brushing by her secretary without a word, Parks
pushed open the door to Brooke's office. Empty.

"I'm sorry, Mr. Jones." The secretary hurried up to
him, warned by the dangerous light in his eye. "Ms.
Gordon . . . Mrs. Jones isn't in."

"Where?" Parks demanded curtly.

"I— Perhaps Ms. Thorton's office. If you'll wait, I'll
check for you. . . ." But he was already heading out
with a long, determined stride that had her chewing on
the nail of her forefinger. It looked like Brooke was in

trouble. And some people have all the luck, the secretary mused before she went back to her desk.

In less than five minutes, Parks walked by the twins in Claire's outer office and opened her door without knocking. "Where's Brooke?" he demanded, not bothering to greet Claire or his agent.

"Good afternoon, Parks," Claire said easily. "Tea?" She continued to pour Lee's cup as if a furious man weren't at that moment glaring at her.

Parks gave the classic little tea service a brief glance. "I'm looking for Brooke."

"You've missed her, I'm afraid." Claire sipped her tea, then offered Lee a plate of macaroons. "She was in and out a half an hour ago. Would you like a cookie, Parks?"

"No. . . ." He managed to get a tenuous hold on his manners. "Thanks. Where did she go?"

Claire nibbled on a macaroon, then dusted her fingers on a pink linen napkin. "Didn't she say she was going home, Lee?"

"Yep. And she wasn't in any better mood than Parks is." He sent his client a bland smile before he wolfed down a cookie.

"No, she wasn't, was she?" Claire folded her hands on her lap. "Tell me, dear, are you two having a tiff?"

"No, we're not having a tiff," Parks muttered, not certain what they were having. It occurred to him suddenly how cozy his agent and his producer were on the small two-cushioned sofa. "What are you two having?" he countered.

"Tea." Claire smiled her dry smile.

"Why don't you have a seat and cool off," Lee invited. "You look like you've just played nine full innings."

"We were shooting on the beach," Parks murmured. Did Lee Dutton have his arm around Claire Thorton, or was he seeing things?

"It went well?" Claire asked, noting his expression, amused by the reason for it.

"Apparently Brooke was satisfied."

"Apparently," Claire murmured, then shot him a level stare. "When are you and Brooke going to relax and enjoy yourselves?"

Parks's speculative look changed to a frown. "What do you mean?"

"I mean I've never in my life seen two people spend so much time poking at each other."

"Is that what you call it?" Parks muttered, stuffing his hands in his pockets.

"For want of a better term." Claire set her teacup carefully in its saucer. "I realize, of course, that the power game is a founding part of your relationship, and provides its own stimulation, but don't you think it's time you became a family as well as opponents?" Keeping her eyes level, Claire settled into the crook of Lee's arm.

Parks stared at her for nearly a full minute. Power game, he repeated silently. Well yes, it was an intricate part of what they were to each other. They had both looked for strength, challenge, and would have walked the other way if they hadn't found the combination. But as for the rest—a family . . . Was that what was niggling at the back of his mind?

Wasn't it true that he couldn't resolve himself to the fact that they were living in *her* house, surrounded by *her* things? He still felt uncomfortably like a guest. Even as fresh annoyance grew, he remembered their discussing a trip to Maui. He had told Brooke he wanted her to see *his* place. But . . . Even as he searched for an excuse, he knew he wouldn't find one.

Turning, Parks paced to the window and scowled out. "I don't think Brooke's ready for a family relationship." The brief, undignified answer Claire gave him had Parks turning back, half-amused. Lee merely reached forward and snatched another cookie.

"She's looked for one all of her life. If you know anything about her, you know that." Suddenly angry, Claire rose. "Is it possible for two people to live together and not understand the other's needs, the other's hurts? How much has she told you about how she grew up?"

"Barely anything," Parks began. "She—"

"How much did you ask?" Claire demanded. "Don't tell me you didn't want to pry," she said quickly, cutting him off. "You're her husband, it's your business to pry. You can be civilized enough to respect her privacy and never touch on what she really needs from you."

"I know that she needs to know she can make her own place," he tossed back. "I know that it doesn't matter if it's a chipped cup or a Hepplewhite table, as long as it's hers."

"Things!" Claire raged. "Yes, she needs things. God knows she never had them as a child, and the child in her still hurts because of it. But they're only a symbol of what she really wants. Brooke walked in here, an eighteen-year-old adult with nothing more than a few dollars in her pocket and a lot of guts. Someone she thought she loved had taken everything from her, and she wasn't ever going to let that happen again.'' Her mouth tightened, her eyes frosting over at the memory. ''It's your job to show her that it won't.''

''I don't want to *take* anything from her,'' Parks retorted heatedly.

''But you want her to give,'' Claire shot back.

''Of course I do, damn it. I love her.''

''Then listen to me. Brooke's struggled all her life to have something of her own, to have some*one* of her own. She has the things. She's earned them. If you want to share them with her, share her life, you'd better have something pretty special to offer in return. Love isn't enough.''

''What is?'' Parks tossed back, furious at being lectured by someone half his size.

''You'd better figure it out.''

Parks measured her another moment. ''All right,'' he said coolly and left without another word.

Lee rose from the sofa to stand beside Claire. Her pampered skin was flushed with temper, her faded blue eyes icy. ''You know,'' he mused as he studied her, ''I've never seen you in full gear before.''

''I don't often lose my temper.'' Claire fluffed at her hair. ''Young people,'' she stated, as if the two words explained everything.

''Yeah.'' Taking her shoulders, he turned her to face him. ''They don't know a good thing when they've got it.'' His puckish round face creased with a grin. ''How'd you like to spend the rest of your life with an overweight theatrical agent?''

The ice melted from Claire's eyes, but the flush remained. "Lee, I thought you'd never ask."

Parks was fighting his way through L.A. traffic when he heard the first report of the fire. His anger at Claire, his frustration that she had spoken no more than the truth, was switched off instantly as he caught the tail end of a news broadcast reporting brush fires in Liberty Canyon—less than an hour away from Brooke's isolated A-frame. No, there wasn't anger now, but a sick sense of fear that had his palms slipping damply on the wheel.

Had she gone home? he wondered frantically as he sped around a cruising Ferrari. Would she have the television set on, the radio, or would she be in one of her solitary moods? After a hot, enervating day on location, she would often simply shower and sleep for an hour. Recharging, he had called it jokingly. Now the idea terrified him.

As he drove higher, he began to scent the fragrance of dry leaves burning. A faint haze of smoke rose into the sky to the east. Thirty minutes, Parks estimated as he pressed his foot on the accelerator. Forty, if they were lucky. It would take him nearly half that to get there.

There was no wind to hurry the fire along, he reminded himself, fighting to keep calm. They weren't calling it a firestorm . . . not yet. Brooke was probably already packing up her most important things—he might even meet her on the road on her way down. Any minute she could come zipping around one of the curves in the road leading back down the mountain. They'd get a hotel, talk this business out. Claire was right, he hadn't dug deep enough. Once he had promised himself he would learn the whole woman. It was long past time to make good on the promise.

Parks could almost taste the smoke now, the thick black smoke that led the way for the fire. He saw a pack of small animals—rabbits, raccoons, a fox—race down the road on the other side in their migration to lower elevation. It was close, then, he thought, too close. Why in God's name wasn't she speeding down the road toward safety? He drove the last fifteen miles in a blur of speed and fear.

Parks only took the time to register that Brooke's car was in the driveway before he was out of his own and racing toward the house. She had to be asleep, he decided, not to know the fire was closing in. Even without the radio on, the haze of smoke and smell of burning brought the news. He burst through the front door, calling her name.

The house was silent. There was no sound of hurried movement, of drawers slamming, nothing to indicate frantic packing. Parks was racing up the stairs two at a time when he heard the dog barking. He swore, but kept going. He'd forgotten the dog completely in his fear for Brooke. And the fear grew again when he saw the bed was empty. He was racing through the second floor, still calling, when a movement outside the window caught his eye.

Rain? he thought, pausing long enough to stare. No, water—but not rain. Going to the window, he saw her. Relief was immediately overlapped by irritation, and irritation by fury. What the hell was she doing standing in the backyard watering the lawn when the smoke was thick enough to block out the trees to the east?

With a quick jerk, he pulled up the window and shouted through the screen. "Brooke, what the hell are you doing?"

She jolted, then looked up. "Oh, Parks, thank God! Come down and help, there isn't much time. Close the window!" she shouted. "The sparks could get inside. *Hurry!*"

He moved, and moved quickly, intending on shaking her until she rattled then dragging her to the car. Halfway down the stairs, he leaped over the banister and headed to the back door. "What the hell are you doing?" he demanded again. Then, instead of shaking her, he found he was holding her tight enough to make her bones crack. If he hadn't heard the radio, if she'd been sleeping . . . *If.* A thousand ifs ran through his mind as his mouth came down frantically on hers.

It was the sudden howl of wind that brought him back. A sudden ripple of terror ran down his spine. The wind would speed the fire and feed the flames. Brush fire became firestorm. "We've got to get out of here."

He had dragged her nearly two feet before he realized she was fighting him. "No!" With a show of pure strength, Brooke broke away from him then picked up the hose she had dropped.

"Damn it, Brooke, we can't have more than fifteen minutes."

He took her arm again and again she broke away. "I know how much time there is." She aimed the spray of water toward the house again, soaking the wood. The sound drummed in the air over the growing fierceness of the wind.

For the first time, Parks noticed that she was wet and filthy and wearing only a bathrobe. She'd just been stepping from the shower when the special report on the radio had warned her of the approaching fire. He looked at the dirt and grass stains on the silk of her robe and realized what she'd been doing. The land around the house had been cleared. She'd done it with her hands. He saw the scratches and dried blood on them and on her legs and ankles. Now, with the puppy barking frantically around her, she was wetting down the house.

"Are you crazy!" he demanded as the first flash of admiration was drowned in fresh fury. Parks grabbed her arm again, ripping the shoulder seam of her robe. "Do you know what a firestorm is?"

"I know what it is." Her elbow connected with his ribs as she struggled away. "If you won't help, stay out of my way; half the house hasn't been wetted down yet."

"You're getting out of here." Parks pulled the hose out of her hand and started dragging her. "If I have to knock you unconscious."

Brooke shocked them both by planting her fist solidly on his jaw. The blow was enough to free her so that she stumbled back, losing her balance and landing on all fours.

"I said stay out of my way," she hissed, then choked as the smoke clogged her lungs.

Parks dragged her to her feet. His eyes were as wild with fear and fury as hers. "You idiot, are you going to fight a firestorm with a garden hose? It's wood and glass!" he shouted as he shook her. "Wood and glass," he repeated, coughing as he threw a hand toward the house. "Is it worth dying for?"

"It's worth fighting for!" she shouted back against smoke and wind as the tears started to flow. "I won't give it to the fire, I *won't!*'' She began fighting him again, more desperately than before.

"Damn it, Brooke, stop!" He took her shoulders until his fingers bit into her flesh. "There isn't time."

"The fire won't have it. Not our home, don't you understand?" Her voice rose, not in hysteria but in fierce determination. "Not *our* home."

Parks stopped shaking her, again finding that his arms had wrapped around to hold her close. Understanding flooded through him, and in its wake came every emotion he'd ever experienced. Is that what Claire had meant, he wondered, when she'd said love wasn't enough? Love was enough for beginning, but sustaining took every feeling a human being was capable of. *Our home*, she had said. And with the two words Brooke had cemented everything.

He drew her away. The tears were streaming, her breath was labored. Her eyes were rimmed with red but steady. He knew he had never felt more for another, and never would. And suddenly he knew that questions and answers weren't necessary for him to know the whole woman. Without speaking, he let her go and picked up the hose himself. Brooke stayed where she was while he turned the water onto the house. With the back of her wrist, she wiped the stinging tears from her face.

"Parks . . ."

He turned, smiling the grim gladiator smile. "It's worth fighting for." Brooke let out a shuddering sigh as she closed her hand over his. "We'll need towels to breathe through, a couple of blankets. Get them while I hose down the rest of the house."

It seemed like hours passed while they worked together, soaking the wood and each other, the dog, again and again while the smoke grew thicker. The wind screamed, threatening to rip the blanket Parks had tossed over her out of her hands. The heat, Brooke thought. She wouldn't be able to bear the heat. But the flames still held off. There were moments she almost believed the fire would veer away, then she would be choking on the smoke and taking her turn with the hose until she couldn't think at all. There was only one goal—to save the house she shared with Parks—the symbol of everything she had ever needed. Home, family, love.

With the towels pressed to their faces, they worked their way around and around the house, soaking the roof, the sides, all the surfaces the heat seemed to dry again so quickly. They no longer spoke, but worked systematically. Two pairs of arms, two sets of legs, working with one mind—to protect what was theirs.

Parks saw the flames first, and was almost too awed to move. It wasn't a furnace, he thought, or an oven. It was hell. And it was racing toward them. Great, greedy towers of fire belched out of the main body like spears. And in the midst of unbearable heat, he felt the icy sweat of human fear.

"No more." In a quick move, he grabbed Brooke's arm and scooped up the puppy.

"What are you doing? We can't leave now." Stumbling and choking, Brooke fought to free herself.

"If we don't leave now, we could be dead." He pushed Brooke into his car and shoved the puppy into her arms. "Damn it, Brooke, we've done all we can." His hands were slick with sweat as he turned the key. "Nothing you can buy is worth dying for."

"You don't understand!" With the back of her hand she smeared grime and tears together on her face. "Everything—everything I have is back there. I can't let the fire take it all—everything that means anything to me."

"Everything," he repeated in a murmur. Parks stopped the car to stare at her with red-rimmed, stinging eyes. "All right, if that's how you feel, I'll go back and do what I can." His voice was curiously flat and emotionless. "But, by God, you stay here. I won't risk you."

Before she could take in what he'd said or what he was doing, he was gone. For a moment, the hysteria had complete control. She trembled with it, unable to move or think. The fire was going to take her home, all her possessions. She'd be left with nothing, just as she had been so many times before. How could she face it again after all the years of struggling, of work, of wanting?

The puppy squirmed in her arms and whimpered. Blankly, Brooke stared down at him. What was she doing sitting there when her house was in danger? She had to go back, go back and save . . . Parks.

Fear froze her, then had her springing from the car and racing through the smoke. She'd sent him back—he'd gone back for her. For what? she thought desperately. What was she trying to save? Wood and glass—that's what he'd called it. It was nothing more. He was her home, the real home she'd searched for all of her life. She shouted for him, sobbing as the smoke blocked everything from view.

She could hear the fire—or the wind. Brooke was no longer certain one was separate from the other. All that was clear was that if she lost him now, she truly lost everything. So she shouted his name again and again, fighting her way through the smoke to get to him.

For an instant she could no longer breathe, no longer be certain where she was or where to run. An image flashed through her mind, one of herself as a young girl approaching a small two-story house where she would spend a year of her life. She couldn't remember the names of the people who would be her parents for those twelve months, only that sense of disorientation and loneliness. She'd always felt as lonely going in as she had coming out. She'd always been separate, always the outsider, until she'd met Parks.

She saw him racing back to her, misted through the curtain of smoke. Before she could separate one image from another, she was in his arms.

"What happened?" he demanded. "I heard you shouting, I thought—" He buried his face against her neck a moment as the fear ebbed. "Damn it, Brooke, I told you to stay in the car."

"Not without you. Please, let's go." She was dragging on his arm, pulling him back down the road toward the car.

"The house—"

"Means nothing," she said fiercely. "Nothing does without you." Before he could react, Brooke was climbing into the driver's seat herself. The moment Parks was beside her, she started down the twisting road.

After nearly a mile, the smoke thinned. It was then Brooke felt the reaction set in with shudders and fresh tears. Pulling off the road, she laid her head on the steering wheel and wept.

"Brooke." Gently, he brushed a hand over her wet, tangled hair. "I'm sorry. I know the house was important to you. We don't know yet that it's gone or beyond repair. We can—''

"Damn the house!" Lifting her head, she looked at him with eyes that were both angry and desolate. "I must've been crazy to act that way. To send you back there when . . ." Trailing off, she swore and slammed out of the car. Slowly, Parks got out and followed her.

"Brooke."

"You're the most important thing in my life." She turned to him then, taking deep breaths to keep the tears back. "I don't expect you to believe that after the way I behaved, but it's true. I couldn't let go of the house, the things, because I'd waited so long to have them. I needed the identity they gave me." Because the words were painful, she swallowed. "For so long everything I had was only mine on loan. All I could think of was that if I didn't keep that house, those things, I'd be lost again. I don't expect you to understand—''

"I will understand." He took her face in his hands. "If you'll let me."

She let out a long, shuddering breath. "I never belonged anywhere, to anyone. Ever. It makes you afraid to trust. I always told myself that there'd be a day when I'd have my own things, my own place—I wouldn't have to share them, I wouldn't have to ask. It was something I promised myself because I couldn't have survived without that one hope. I forgot to let go of that when I didn't need it anymore."

"Maybe." He stroked a thumb over her cheek. "Or maybe you had without realizing it. Back there, you called it *our* home."

"Parks." She reached up to place her hands on him. "I don't care if the house is gone, if everything in it's gone. I have everything I need, everything I love, right here in my hands.''

They were wet, filthy, exhausted. Alive. Parks looked at her blackened face and matted hair, the red-rimmed eyes. She'd never looked more beautiful to him. Throats raw from smoke, eyes stinging, he reached for her. Together, they fell to the grass.

Brooke was laughing and weeping as he kissed her. Her face was streaked with soot and tears, but his lips raced wildly over it. Passion met passion. Bruises were unfelt as they touched each other while a need, as volatile as the fire they had challenged, raged through them. When the tatters of her robe were gone, his sodden clothes joining it, they lay tangled, naked on the grass. Again and again, their mouths clung, drawing the strength and victory of the moment from each other, climbing beyond the smoke and stench of the fire left behind to a clean, bright world.

She knew she had never been so aware, so stunningly alive. Her body seemed to hum from a thousand pulses that grew more erratic as he touched her. With her arms tight around him, his body pressed against hers, she felt the sensation of absolute trust. He would protect, she would defend, against any outside forces that threatened. During the fire, they had ceased to be a man and a woman. They had become a unit. Somewhere beneath the swirling passion, Brooke felt peace. She had found her own.

They made love while the smoke broke into mists above their heads. And when they were spent, they clung still, unwilling to break the unity so newly discovered.

''You've hurt yourself,'' Parks murmured, touching a bruise on her shoulder.

"I don't feel hurt." She buried her lips at his throat and knew she would never forget the smell of smoke and ash and loving. "I hit you."

"Yeah, I noticed."

Hearing the grin in his voice, she closed her eyes. "You were only thinking of me. I'm sorry."

"Now you're thinking of us." He pressed his lips to her temple. "I'm glad."

"We won," she whispered.

Parks lifted his head to look down at her. Taking his thumb, he rubbed a streak of soot from her skin. It was the color of her eyes, he thought, seeing it on his own flesh. "We won, Brooke."

"Everything."

His lips curved before he brought them down to hers. "Everything."

She cradled his head on her shoulder, gently stroking his hair. Tiny pieces of ash continued to float above her like memories. "I said once I didn't want anything to change. . . . I was afraid to let it change. I was wrong." Closing her eyes, she let herself absorb his closeness. "It's not quite the same now."

"Better," he murmured. "It makes a difference. It'll always make a difference."

She sighed, knowing the contentment she had always searched for was irrevocably bound up in one man, one love. "But we'll still play the game, won't we?"

This time when he lifted his head, he grinned. Brooke's lips curved in response. "By our own rules."

If you enjoyed this book...

Thrill to 4 more
Silhouette Intimate Moments
novels (a $9.00 value)—
ABSOLUTELY FREE!

If you want more passionate sensual romance, then Silhouette Intimate Moments novels are for you!

In every 256-page book, you'll find romance that's electrifying...involving... and intense. And now, these larger-than-life romances can come into your home every month!

4 FREE books as your introduction.

Act now and we'll send you four thrilling Silhouette Intimate Moments novels. They're our gift to introduce you to our convenient home subscription service. Every month, we'll send you four new Silhouette Intimate Moments books. Look them over for 15 days. If you keep them, pay just $9.00 for all four. Or return them at no charge.

We'll mail your books to you *as soon as they are published.* Plus, with every shipment, you'll receive the Silhouette Books Newsletter absolutely free. *And Silhouette Intimate Moments is delivered free.*

Mail the coupon today and start receiving Silhouette Intimate Moments. Romance novels for women...not girls.

Silhouette Intimate Moments

Silhouette

Intimate Moments

more romance, more excitement

$2.25 each

Silhouette

Intimate 🖤 *Moments*

more romance, more excitement

Silhouette Intimate Moments

Coming Next Month

THE REAL MAN
by Alexandra Sellers

•

EVERYTHING BUT TIME
by Mary Lynn Baxter

•

WINNER'S CIRCLE
by April Thorne

•

BITTERSWEET RAIN
by Erin St. Claire

For the woman who expects a little more out of love, get Silhouette Special Edition.

Take 4 books free — no strings attached.

If you yearn to experience more passion and pleasure in your romance reading ... to share even the most private moments of romance and sensual love between spirited heroines and their ardent lovers, then Silhouette Special Edition has everything you've been looking for.

Get 6 books each month before they are available anywhere else!

Act now and we'll send you four exciting Silhouette Special Edition romance novels. They're our gift to introduce you to our convenient home subscription service. Every month, we'll send you six new passion-filled Special Edition books. Look them over for 15 days. If you keep them, pay just $11.70 for all six. Or return them at no charge.

We'll mail your books to you *two full months before they are available* anywhere else. Plus, with every shipment, you'll receive the Silhouette Books Newsletter absolutely free. *And with Silhouette Special Edition there are never any shipping or handling charges.*

Mail the coupon today to get your four free books — and more romance than you ever bargained for.

Silhouette Special Edition is a service mark and a registered trademark of Simon & Schuster, Inc.